Stories From Bondi

Also by Libby Sommer and published by Ginninderra Press
My Year with Sammy
The Crystal Ballroom
The Usual Story

Libby Sommer

Stories From Bondi

Susanne Gervay OAM
Thank you for believing in me.

Thanks to Silda Trainor, Toni Grunseit, Ruth Moss, Toni Paramore,
Women Writers Network.

Stories From Bondi
ISBN 978 1 76041 790 1
Copyright © Libby Sommer 2019
Cover: Shutterstock

First published 2019 by
GINNINDERRA PRESS
PO Box 3461 Port Adelaide 5015
www.ginninderrapress.com.au

Contents

Art and the Mermaid

Once upon a time it came to pass, so it is said, that an enormous storm swept the coast of New South Wales, doing extensive damage to the ocean beaches – destroying jetties, breakwaters and washing away retaining walls. Mountainous seas swept Bondi Beach and dashed against the cliffs, carrying ruin with every roller. At North Bondi near Ben Buckler, a huge submerged block of sandstone weighing 233 tons was lifted ten feet and driven 160 feet to the edge of the cliff, where it remains to this day.

One day, a Sydney sculptor, Lyall Randolph, looked upon the rock and was inspired. The sculptor was a dreamer. Let us, he said, have two beautiful mermaids to grace the boulder. Using two Bondi women as models, he cast the two mermaids in fibreglass and painted them in gold.

Without council approval and at his own expense, he erected *The Mermaids* for all to see on the giant rock that had been washed up by the sea. *The Mermaids* sat side by side on the rock. One shaded her eyes as she scanned the ocean and the other leant back in a relaxed fashion with an uplifted arm sweeping her hair up at the back of her neck. Their fishy tails complemented the curves and crevices of their bodies.

It so happened that less than a month after *The Mermaids* were put in place, one was stolen and damaged. The council held many meetings to decide if she should be replaced using ratepayers' money. The council had previously objected to the sculptor placing the statues there without council permission. The sculptor had argued that before placing *The Mermaids* in position he had taken all necessary steps to obtain the requisite permission.

The large boulder at Ben Buckler, upon which *The Mermaids* were securely bolted and concreted, he said, is not in the municipality of Waverley at all. It is in the sea. According to the Australian Constitution, the high-tide mark is the defined limit of the Waverley Council's domain. The Maritime Services Board and the Lands Department both advised me they had no objection to the erection of *The Mermaids*.

One Waverley alderman said he wished both mermaids had been taken instead of only one. Someone else said the sculptor didn't need the council's permission to put them there in the first place and *The Mermaids* had given Bondi a great attraction without any cost to the council. The sculptor said *The Mermaids* had brought great publicity to the council. They had been featured in films, newspapers, television and the *National Geographic* magazine.

The mayor used his casting vote in favour of the mermaid and she was reinstalled.

For over ten years, the two beautiful golden mermaids reclined at Ben Buckler, attracting many thousands of sightseers to the beach.

Poised on the huge boulder, they braved the driving storms of winter until one day one was washed off. The council saw its opportunity and removed the other.

Today, only the remnants of one mermaid remain – but not on the rock. In a glass cabinet in Waverley Library at Bondi Junction, all that is left of the two beautiful mermaids is a figure with half a face. There's a hole instead of a cheek, a dismembered torso, part of an uplifted arm, the tender groove of an armpit. And there, down below, a complete fish's tail.

After the Rain

Just before six o'clock on Friday evening, Anny and Gordon get out of Anny's Honda. They walk down Bondi Road passing the tattoo shop, the vegetarian restaurant and yet another new Thai restaurant. The road is unusually quiet and Anny has parked directly opposite the fish café where she's taking Gordon for dinner. The streets aren't gridlocked during the Olympics after all and there's an unusual calm on this usually noisy busy road.

Walk in front of me, says Gordon as they head towards the traffic lights and the pedestrian crossing. I can see better if you walk slightly in front of me.

She doesn't know whether to offer him her arm or what. She feels embarrassed at the thought of close physical contact with him and is pleased that he's told her to walk in front. At least she knows now the best way to progress along the street with him. Not like the snail's pace of the week before.

Anny's friend had rung and asked Anny to help out by taking Gordon for a walk or a movie or something – to help keep him entertained for the four weeks of his visit during the Olympics.

If he's halfway decent, I'll let you know, said the friend's wife.

Don't worry, said Anny, I'll take him out anyway.

Tonight he's wearing jeans and a cream shirt. At least he's not wearing joggers and that bright jacket in loud primary colours that he wore last time. Tonight, Anny has dressed down. She took the time to have a bath and change out of her work clothes before picking him up. She's wearing dark brown suede trousers and a lemon cotton singlet top with matching cardigan – a colour that suits her dark hair and pale skin well enough when she is at her best, but she is not at her best today. She is wearing dark glasses, and the reason is that she has taken to weeping in spurts, never at the really bad times but in between; the spurts are as unbidden as sighs.

Before her first outing with Gordon, she worried so much about escorting a visually impaired man that when she arrived home from work she'd prayed that the one message on her answer machine would be from her friend saying the arrangement to go out was cancelled. This time as she stands at her mirror preparing to go out, she feels good to be dressing for a date. It will be nice to go out for a meal, even though she has to pick him up and usher him around. He hadn't seemed that bad. Maybe she'll bring him back to her place afterwards. They could have a drink, she could show him the view down the gully – the jungle of vines and palms and ferns – maybe even hear the birds in the morning.

Standing at her dressing table, she sees reflected in the glass the tree at the top of the gully – she doesn't know its name – its twisted gnarled branches, a variety of greens in its leaves, the occasional red bloom amongst the foliage – the one the cockatoos like to eat. It's draped against the red-tiled roof of the house in front. The Pacific Ocean behind. The terracotta roofs and the blue of the ocean remind her of living on the French Riviera with a glimpse of the Mediterranean from her studio window, blue behind the red roof in front of her. A little corner of blue. She'd been able to live happily alone then: without a man, without a car, without a regular job. Occasional commissions. When she came back to Australia, she thought she'd get more commissions. And why hasn't she? No time, not enough light, nowhere to work, too isolating. The familiar self-pity – she recognises it as self-pity – rises in her like bitter bile.

It's only a short drive to her friend's house in Surry Hills.

You wouldn't know there's anything wrong with him, her friend had said on the phone. Slight brain damage from a New York mugging.

She parks directly outside the house so he can step straight into the passenger side of the car when she opens the door for him. He uses the handle at the side of the seat to move his seat back.

I hope it's not too cramped for you there, she says.

No problem. I used to drive a sports car. I'm used to it.

Now Anny and Gordon cross Bondi Road at the lights and head towards the liquor store. Anny suggested they buy a bottle of wine to drink with dinner. She's booked a table at the fish restaurant because he said that's what he likes to eat.

They walk into the restaurant, Gordon carrying the Pinot, Anny leading the way. White tablecloths, white crockery, black-lacquered chairs. White butcher paper in sheets on top of the white cloths. No opportunity to illustrate signature table mats in here, thinks Anny. Not like the cafés on the waterfront in the south of France with their unique architectural styles. The waitress, uniformed in a black apron over black T-shirt and trousers, leads them to the back of the restaurant, away from the television screen with the Olympics and closer to the ambient background music. The fake strelitzia replaced at the front of the restaurant by the television set.

Gordon excuses himself and goes to the toilet. I'm glad he's able to find his way to the toilet unaided, she thinks. And strangely enough he could read the $1.20 corkage charge in minute writing at the bottom of the menu.

A man and a woman at the next table finish their meal and leave. The table is quickly cleaned up. The white paper on the tablecloth removed and replaced.

From the kitchen, a waitress brings a jug of water with ice cubes and slices of lemon and places two glasses on the table. She picks up the bottle of wine. Do you want it on ice or room temperature? she asks.

Room temperature would be fine.

When Gordon returns from the toilet, he pours the red wine into her glass and then into his own. They lift their glasses towards each other but neither of them proposes a toast. They settle back in their chairs. The sound of the Olympic games swimming excitement carries up to their end of the restaurant. They share a green salad and thick Italian bread as they wait for their meal.

So you're collecting grandchildren? says Gordon.

Anny is not pleased at this question. Surely he can think of something else to ask her apart from grandchildren. She loves her little grandchild of course but she's still a bit reticent about shouting out to the world that she's now a grandmother. He's asked the question in such a way that it sounds like a statement, so she sees no reason to reply.

How many have you got? he persists.

Just the one, indicating by her tone of voice that that's where the matter ends for now.

She couldn't help but look into his mouth and see his little yellowed receding teeth and his thin lips as he used his finger to wedge out pieces of stuck fish at the side of his mouth. There's a grain of rice on his cheek next to his mouth and she wonders whether to say anything, but luckily it falls off as he takes another bite of his barramundi.

Although there are fans on the ceiling, it's very hot in the restaurant. Anny wants to take off her cardigan but she doesn't want to expose her arms, her upper arms that is, that are less than perfect even though she does weights and other things at the gym.

She wears a jacket or a cardigan always now to draw the eyes and attention away from that part of her body that is growing larger at a more rapid rate than the rest of her, which is causing her much alarm. You'd think that with all the exercise she did her body wouldn't be so out of control. She never thought this would happen to her. She thought she'd be spared the disgrace and indignity of it all. Other women say they've had enough of the messy monthly bleeding and are happy to take a tablet that stops the flow. But then she also knows women who say they've had enough of sex too – that messy business. So, we're not all the same, she reminds herself.

When Anny and Gordon finish eating, Gordon wants to order a coffee straight away and keeps looking around for the waitress.

The service isn't as good as it was when we first arrived, he says.

The waitress probably thinks we want to take it slowly rather than rush in, eat and leave in the quickest possible time, she says.

Eventually the waitress brings a latte and a short black with a mint chocolate on the side of each saucer.

Anny offers to pay but he tells her she can leave the tip.

Will you come in? he asks when she drops him back to her friend's front door.

No thanks. I've got an early start tomorrow.

He looks disappointed and she tries not to feel bad as she watches him walk to the security gate and let himself in with his key.

She goes through her morning ritual of watering her herbs on the balcony. Takes the coriander and parsley out of their containers so the water can run off from the roots so they won't get pot bound. She keeps them in ceramic pots on an old oak hallstand that she keeps on the balcony. There was nowhere else to fit the treasured hallstand after moving into a unit from the house where she lived with her children. She thought when the children left home she'd do so many of the things she never had time for before. But she doesn't.

She keeps the beloved hallstand outside at the mercy of the elements – although under cover. She just has to remember to keep it well oiled. And it is providing a suitable place to grow herbs. Not that she's a gardener. But she's pretending to be happy. She's trying hard to be happy. Growing herbs seems like a good thing to do.

She'd like to buy a rocket plant as well. When she lived in Europe, she ate a lot of rocket. Especially in Italy. But the rocket plants in the garden centre at Bondi Junction have small light green leaves.

Is this the only rocket plant you have in here? Anny asks the young woman who comes up to serve her at the garden centre.

Yes. And you'll have to repot it into a larger container.

Anny uses the opportunity to ask if she should repot her parsley and coriander plants.

Yes, definitely the parsley. I don't know about coriander.

As the woman speaks, Anny looks into her pale unadorned face, sees her short plain hair, her apron over her overalls and wonders if she's gay. Working in a garden centre would be a good job for a gay woman, thinks Anny.

You can bring in your parsley and coriander plants and I'll repot them for you, she says. There'll be no charge for my time. Only the cost of the pot and the potting mix.

I'll come back another day when I've got my car.

That's a good idea, says the woman with a smile.

It always worries Anny when gay women smile at her.

She thanks the woman as a buzzer rings from inside the centre for the third time since they'd been speaking together.

*

I'm feeling nervous and anxious and stressing out about taking this fellow out again tonight to the Opera House, Anny says to her daughter on the telephone. I was trying to do a kind deed but now I wish I hadn't offered. I have to race home from work, eat, get the car, pick him up, find out how to park at the Opera House, manoeuvre him in, et cetera, et cetera, all before seven-thirty.

Don't worry, Mum. You worried last time and you managed. You'll manage okay this time. Okay?

It's raining. The ocean churned up and mottled with waves. The whole expanse of the sky grey with no definition between clouds and sky furring in with the sea. The waterfall at the top of the gully thunders relentlessly.

Anny closes the sliding door against the huge sound of water torrenting down rocks. She watches through the glass the leaves of the pot plants blowing in the wind. She remembers feeling lighter than this. Remembers not being weighted down with tears at the back of her eyes. Remembers being without this hole in her stomach. It's not always like this, she reminds herself.

The double-glazed glass deadens the noise. She turns the radio news down now that she is cushioned from the sound of the rain and walks to her desk. On the table, a sketch of a mermaid wearing a bra.

No pubic hair and no nipples are her instructions for this children's book.

As Anny and Gordon drive to the Opera House, Anny thinks about what annoys her the most about him. Probably that he doesn't remember things that she tells him. For example, on every outing so far he's asked if she's travelled.

Travelled outside the country, I mean, Gordon says now in the car.

Yes, I've travelled lots.

Where have you been?

Just about everywhere.

You'd think he'd remember this bit of significant detail about her and her life. But each time she's seen him, he asks her the same question. And the other big problem is his loud American voice. When they're out, everyone around them can hear what he's saying. And then when she says something and lowers her voice, he says, What? in a loud voice.

What did you say? he repeats.

She's stopped initiating conversation.

So then he keeps saying, Well?

Well? he'll say for no apparent reason when she's driving or they're walking along the street. He says it now as they drive towards the Opera House.

Well?

Silence.

She's concentrating on her driving and worried about finding somewhere to park.

Well then? he says by way of a variation.

Looking at Gordon sideways as he stands there silhouetted by the Harbour Bridge on the forecourt of the Opera House, the wings of the Opera House behind him, she can see from his profile that he was probably quite handsome once. Defined cheekbones, regular features, a strength in his face, and probably he had a decent physique. Tonight he wears dark blue corduroys and a pale blue denim shirt open at the neck and brown American-style loafers. At least he's not wearing one of those horrible navy blue blazers with gold buttons that most men his age seem to wear for special occasions.

Gordon looks over at the sign pointing to the Drama Theatre. At least they know how to spell theatre here in Australia, he comments. Not like the Americans.

She nods.

He probably isn't even aware that she's not speaking to him. In the theatre, he talks to the man in the seat at the end of the row. Tells the man he's here visiting from America for the Olympics. Now he's talking to the man about theatre on Broadway and off Broadway.

I used to go to the theatre, says Gordon wistfully. But not recently. Not since I lost my wife.

As they sit watching *Troilus and Cressida*, she can't help but notice his sniffing, like a tic, a regular involuntary sniff. And then there he is asleep, first on one armrest leaning to the right and then on the other armrest leaning in her direction. She worries that he'll fall over or down in his chair and she'll have to wake him up or, worse still, that his whole body will fall across on to her.

There was a lot of nudity in that play, she says to Gordon as she drives him home. I hadn't realised when I booked the tickets that there'd be so much nudity.

Yes, he says.

Judging by *Troilus and Cressida*, nudity and sex is back in – in the theatre, she says. Breasts and bottoms everywhere, she thinks. Jiggling bottoms. You can only see so much of jiggling bottoms. I can see the need for wardrobe. Wardrobe and make-up.

There are more accidents on the road on rainy days, he says looking out the window. People get more frustrated.

They drive up Macquarie Street, across William Street, into Oxford Street and then right into York Road on the eastern side of Centennial Park. Then into Birrell Street and right into Bronte Road, winding around the roundabouts, straight down the hill past the palm trees and the ocean and are rounding the corner to turn into Macpherson Street. It is a narrow road, not well lit and not used much in the evening. Coming down Macpherson Street from the west is a Lithuanian cyclist in training to compete in the Olympic women's road cycling in a week's time. She arrived in Sydney that afternoon and is having a practice ride on the Centennial Park to Bronte route. She doesn't know, or she's forgotten, that cars drive on the other side of the road in Australia. She's approaching the corner of Macpherson Street and Bronte Road cycling fast down the hill at between sixty and seventy kilometres an hour on the wrong side of the road, and she's hasn't any lights.

There isn't time to say a word. Gordon doesn't yell out. Anny doesn't touch the brake. The bike and rider flash before them, like a huge seabird heading straight for the windows of a plane, smashing into glass. The cyclist comes down the dark street and fills the air straight towards Anny, gliding into view of the headlights. And then she's gone – she's disappeared around the corner and into the lights of Bronte Road.

What Anny feels is not terror or thanksgiving – not yet. What she feels is something else. A lightness – as disconnected from previous and future events as the woman on the bike was, the black bird.

Gordon speaks first. That was close, and then, with his hand on the door he says, I won't ask you to come in. I know you've got an early start tomorrow.

She nods, then turns the car around and drives home. She puts the car away in the lock-up garage and walks up the internal stairs and out on to the balcony. She turns towards the sea looking for the position of the moon tonight. There it is up to her left. The knotty branches of the flame tree move overhead, and under these branches the moonlight comes through on to the weathered hallstand, on to her newly potted herbs and on to her new home.

She inhales deeply the sweet clear smell of trees after rain. The gentle flow of the waterfall. The dribbling of moisture off branches and leaves. The cleansing bright spike of air.

She smiles to herself as she thinks of tomorrow afternoon, when she'll see her granddaughter again. She'll lie on the floor and let the baby use her as a climbing tower. She'll haul herself up to a standing position using Anny's body for support and then Anny will watch her crawl away to explore every surface of the room, to pull and shake and rattle and examine with her little fat fingers every interesting movable object in her path.

Around Midnight

'When are you open?' Anny asks the woman on the telephone.

'We have a party twice a day. Every day. Twelve-thirty to four-thirty and seven-thirty to midnight.'

'Oh. Every day? I thought it was Saturday nights only.'

'No, darling. Every day.'

'So what's the set-up?'

'Hundred and twenty dollars for a couple. Nothing if you come on your own. What's your position? How would you come along?'

'On my own.'

'It would cost you nothing then.'

'But what do you do? I mean, I know what goes on there.'

'You've been here before?'

'No. A friend told me about it. What do you wear? What's the set-up?'

'It's all up to you, love. If you fancy a gentleman, you invite him into one of the rooms.'

'What do you wear, though? My friend said something about robes.'

'Towels. They're towels, love. You wear whatever you like. Normal clothes.'

Anny is sitting at a café at North Bondi having breakfast with her friend Dita telling her about it. Anny has ordered the scrambled tofu and Dita is having fried eggs and bacon.

I'm dying to know how you went, Dita says, pulling her chair closer to the table.

Well, Anny says, this is what happened.

It's eight-thirty on Saturday night when I approach a big steel gate with a street number in bold letters. I open the gate and go up the lane way beside the Thai restaurant and follow the fairy lights upstairs. There's nothing else to indicate what goes on inside this three-bedroom apartment on a busy road in Bondi. I follow the fairy lights along a corridor until I come to a wooden front door with no number on it. I hesitate, not knowing whether to knock or just walk in. I open the door.

Inside, draped around the room, are about ten men and women in various stages of undress sitting on stools beside small bar tables – the men bare-chested, the women topless or wearing bras. Some of them are giving each other neck and shoulder massages. And they're all wearing towels. Not a very attractive sight, in my opinion – a man in a towel.

It's a large room with a pretend-bar, a kitchen on the right and sliding glass doors that lead to a covered balcony with an above-ground spa pool. Standing by the door are two Japanese men in black jeans and black T-shirts. I walk over to the kitchen, which acts as the reception area.

The only other fully dressed people in the room are the man and the woman who run the place. She's Czech, young and very attractive in a green lace figure-revealing dress. Her blonde hair cascades down her back. She's in the kitchen and doesn't exactly greet me but asks me what I'd like to drink.

A glass of wine would be nice, I say.

She goes to the fridge and from a cask on the bottom shelf pours me a glass. With drink in hand, I stand near the door and look around. And wonder what I'll do next.

The two Japanese men avoid eye contact with me. They obviously want to keep to themselves. I don't particularly want to join the group of men and women on the stools as I don't intend to take any of my clothes off.

I ask the woman who runs the place to show me around. She

shrugs without much enthusiasm then leads the way along a narrow hallway. The first bedroom on the right has a double bed with a bedside light on a table and white lace curtains on the window. She looks out between the lace peering around outside before pulling them closed. She shows me another bedroom at the end of the corridor with an en suite bathroom. We stand at the door looking in to the empty bed but she doesn't show me in. And then she leads the way to the third bedroom back along the corridor towards the front door.

This is the Orgy Room, she says from the open doorway.

I avert my eyes but I can see from the corner of one eye a double bed and several naked bodies doing things to each other. Backs and thighs and bums exposed. Not very becoming. It all seems tacky and I begin to doubt my wisdom in coming to a place like this. I clutch my handbag across my body and find myself a seat in the front room with my back to the wall.

There are corn chips and an onion dip on a platter that the women in the group hand around. I decline the chips and the dip. If there's one thing I can't stand, it's the smell of onion breath.

A woman in a white lace bra and a towel around her waist stubs out her cigarette in the ashtray in front of me and asks if I've been here before.

No, I say. And you?

I come here all the time. What do you do for a living? she continues.

A bit of this and that.

She nods knowingly.

What do you do? I ask.

I'm a psychologist at a clinic at St Leonards.

I'm very surprised. For some reason, I thought women with important jobs wouldn't come to a place like this.

A man edges over towards me and tries to get in on our conversation. He asks the same things as she does. Do you come here often? What do you do for a living?

In the old days, or, rather, in the olden days, as my children like to say, when I used to frequent bars from time to time, I'd answer the first question with 'only in the mating season' and the second with 'I live off the income from my investments'. Both replies would be met with a stunned silence or an impressed 'ah' or, sometimes, 'is this the mating season?'

The man keeps smiling at me and I avert my eyes but somehow he is able to manoeuvre himself around so he's constantly in my line of vision. It gives me the shits.

Not your type? Dita puts in.

No. Absolutely not.

What did you wear in the end? Dita asks.

Only four items of clothing.

Something you could take off quickly?

Yes. And no jewellery. Apparently the men have to shower and put on a towel as soon as they arrive. Although one woman kept saying to me, where's your towel? She wanted me to get undressed and hang about in a towel like everyone else.

Another woman tells me I should leave my bag locked up in the kitchen with the man and woman who own the place. You don't know these men, cautions the woman. Lock up your bag.

I decide to keep my bag with me, although I've left my umbrella beside the door.

Another man edges his stool over towards me and we have a conversation. At least he's got a brain in his head and got something to say for himself. He tells me he's Dutch and he's here in Sydney on business.

It's my first time to this place, he says. But I've been to others in other cities in the world. I travel a lot for business.

We talk a little about travel and countries we've visited.

He lets me know in a non-threatening way that he'd be willing to go into one of the bedrooms with me. I feel embarrassed knocking him back seeing as we've had such a nice conversation and I don't want him to be wasting time with me if he wants to be chatting up some other woman.

I'm not ready, I say politely. Maybe later.

The other man who's been trying to catch my eye, the pain-in-the-bum-persistent-dag who listens in to my every word, leans over towards me and says, When you're ready, would you go into one of the rooms with me?

No thanks, I say. Sorry, I smile at him, hoping all the same that I haven't hurt his feelings.

The Dutch man tells me there's no need to apologise.

A few new people wander in. A man and a woman, a couple, a few single men of various ages and shapes and a fat girl draped in layers of chiffon. Then two very well-proportioned young men. I remind myself that I'm the one meant to be doing the choosing here. One of the very well-proportioned young men is quite cute actually. The other young man is not very tall, a bit too muscle-bound for my taste, and has that short spiky hair almost-shaved-at-the-side that I find most unattractive. The two of them are younger than my son – but that's nothing new.

One of the women ushers them out into the back bedroom to shower and put on a towel. They don't return to the main room, where I'm sitting jammed up between various men and in front of me a blank video screen high up on the wall. The fat girl does some sort of disco dance in front of the wall under the video screen. She dances in time to the music but nothing special. Then the woman who owns the place uses her remote to turn on a video.

I've never seen such an explicit porn video before, Dita. I can't watch but I glimpse the extreme close-ups of women's genitalia and pierced intimate body parts and things being stuck in and up and it's all too horrible.

Why didn't you go home then? Asks Dita.

I thought I'd wait just a bit longer. It had taken such an enormous effort of will to get there.

The Czech blonde who runs the place with her Indian husband enjoys the video immensely. Look at that, she keeps saying.

I have nowhere to turn my head. In front of me the video, to my left the persistent dag. To my right is the smaller young muscly man who now also keeps trying to attract my attention, but I'm claustrophobic and I just want out of there but for some reason I'm stuck to my seat. I don't want to stand up and have everyone look at me – anything that moves is closely observed in this room. I look at the floor, at the space between my stool and the spa area, and the floor towards the front door. I'm willing myself to stand up, to walk into the spa room away from these men, or straight out the front door.

So that's how come I end up talking to the young Italian muscly bloke. He reaches his hand out to me and invites me to sit in the spa room with him away from the noise of the video. I use his hand to stand up but then remove it from his grasp before walking outside to the balcony. I don't want to look as if I've been claimed.

I tell the muscly Italian man that the men here are too predatory and I'm feeling guilty because I keep knocking them back and then find myself apologising. You don't have to apologise when you knock someone back, he assures me. But I'm finding him intimidating right now wedged up beside me and I don't know how to get rid of him.

We sit on the black vinyl lounge, me squashed in the corner beside him. The tang of chlorine from the empty spa assaults my nostrils.

Can I kiss your cheek? he asks.

No.

Can I hold your hand? he says.

No. I wedge my hand that lays beside him under my thigh making sure he can't hold it.

His friend, the cutie, comes out through the door and sits beside us. We smile at each other.

I was very nervous before coming to this place, he says to me. I nearly didn't come.

I look into his open face and his nice round eyes and thick head of curly hair.

It was the same for me, I say.

When I came in, he says, I saw you sitting there and that woman in the green dress and I thought this looks all right and so I came in.

She's very attractive, I say. That woman in the green dress.

I asked her husband if she participates but he said no.

Do you think it's good value for money here? I ask in order to keep the conversation going. I mean it's concerning me that the men have paid $180 each to come into this place and it's free for me.

No, he says, I don't think I've got good value for money. Not so far.

His friend puts his hand on my leg. I consider removing his hand but think it may seem churlish of me so I don't. And anyway if I've come to a place like this, what am I doing knocking all the blokes back?

What does it cost to have sex with a hooker? I ask the cutie.

He looks at me with horrified wide eyes. I don't know. I've never had sex with a hooker.

I was just trying to do a price comparison. A value for money price comparison.

How many women have you had sex with tonight? I persist.

Two. One on arrival. A woman started massaging me when I had a shower and then we had sex. And then a second one almost straight afterwards. The fat girl.

How was that? I ask. How was the sex?

She had big bruises all over her body as if she'd been bashed up or drugs or something. Her arms and legs were all bruised. It was awful. I wished I was unconscious.

I nod with sympathy. I noticed you go into the bedroom with the fat girl, I say.

He smiles at me and extends his hands towards me, palms upturned. I could give you a great massage, he says with enthusiasm. I've got very strong hands. I'm trained in martial arts.

Mm, I say breathing out with a sigh.

But the problem is I can't get rid of his bloody friend. He's latched on to me and has territorial control with his bloody hand resting on my thigh.

There are six of us in the spa room now. The cutie, his friend, a middle-aged Maori couple and the Indian husband of the Czech woman. I'd noticed some of the girls flirting with the Indian husband and then laughing. He stays close by the side of his wife. Now, though, he chats to us.

We've only had this business for eight weeks, he says. We took it over from the previous owner, who'd been here for six and a half years. It costs us $1,000 a month in rent and $1,000 for advertising on the web, in the *Telegraph* and in the *Wentworth Courier*. It isn't easy to make money.

We talk about business and making money for a while then he leaves us to it.

Do you think some of those girls are being paid to be here? asks the Italian.

Prostitutes?

Well, why would a single woman come to a place like this? says the cutie who's disappointed there aren't more women here. A single woman can go out any time and pick up a bloke at a pub.

I don't say anything. I don't say it's probably safer here than to take a stranger home or to go back to his place in the middle of nowhere. And what are you meant to do anyway if you don't have a boyfriend?

He complains that when he rang up to make inquiries they told him there is a huge spa that fits twenty people. They could fit about eight people in this spa, he says. And even then it would be squashed. Twenty people – they'd all be on top of each other.

I must say that when my friend Richard, who told me about the place, mentioned that there is a large spa I did imagine a Grecian-type setting with women and men reclining and relaxing around the edges of the water.

If he was a good businessman, says the cutie, he'd offer to give us our money back at the door. That's how you do business. Keep the customers happy.

There's no privacy in the rooms here, says the Italian. People walk in all the time. The Japanese men paid $50 each just to watch.

We had to jam towels up against the door to stop people walking in, says the Maori husband.

Now that the Maori couple have joined in the conversation, I use the opportunity to ask them how they're going. What they've experienced so far. I'd noticed them come out of the bedroom at the end of the house.

The wife tells me in a quiet voice that they went into the room with another woman to have a threesome. But it didn't work out, she says. He couldn't do any good, she says indicating with a nod her husband's lap and the area between his legs. We don't like it much here. We've been to other singles clubs where it's all couples. Much better. Not with all these men hanging around staring at you.

Why did you come here? I ask.

He wants to have sex with other women. So coming to a place like this, he's not doing it behind my back. I know what he's up to and I'm included.

Her husband glows smugly.

Why did you come here? I ask the cutie.

Curiosity. Why did you come here? he asks me.

Curiosity. We all came here for curiosity, I say, summing up the conversation.

The Italian muscle-man gets up to go to the toilet. Save me that space beside you, he instructs me. Promise, he adds loudly.

I nod.

When he leaves the room, I ask the cutie if he's been into the Orgy Room.

No, he says. What Orgy Room?

It's up the hallway. I had a look around when I arrived. But an Orgy Room isn't something I'm interested in trying.

Me either, he agrees. I'm just waiting for him to finish with you, he says, indicating the empty seat between us, and then I'll be next.

I lower my eyes discreetly and suppress a smirk.

The Italian returns from the toilet and takes his seat between us.

The cutie turns to me and says, You can give him a massage, indicating his friend, and I'll give you a massage.

I laugh.

The Maori couple encourage me from the sidelines.

Go on, says the Maori husband. Give it a go. If you don't like it, leave.

Sure, I think to myself. As if I'd be able to leave after going into a bedroom with two men and taking off all my clothes. Although I wouldn't mind going in to one of the rooms with the cutie, if I could lock the door, that is, and if it wasn't so late already.

I giggle nervously. I have four people on my case now trying to persuade me to go with the two young men, as if it's my responsibility to keep everybody happy. Hoping they'll understand and lay off, I tell them I'm laughing because I'm nervous.

Would a drink calm you down? says the husband.

No thanks.

His wife smiles at me. In a gentle voice she says, Would you like me to calm you down?

Thank you very much, but no, I say, feeling guilty as usual.

Her husband makes some more noises along the lines of the two of them could help me out with my nervousness problem.

I sigh and then stand up brushing the hand off my leg. I walk over to the side of the spa where the cutie is standing. I ease two fingers into the water as if to test the temperature. Warm, I say.

Not warm enough, he says.

I move towards him then lift the corner of his towel to just above his knee. I dry my fingers.

His friend jumps up from the lounge and moves in front of me with his bare hairy back just inches from my face. My back is cold, he says. Warm me up, he commands.

I hold out one hand and lay it briefly on his shoulder, then take it away.

Let's go for a walk, he whispers to me.

No thanks.

Give me your phone number and we'll meet up another time then.

No.

Why not?

I don't want to. I laugh nervously. How I hate these situations I find myself in.

I'm now wedged into the corner of the spa room. My eyes fix on the door. I hesitate, wondering whether I should be polite and say anything to the Maori couple. But I feel the need for haste. I'm worried he'll follow me, although a man in a towel isn't going to get very far outside on the street.

Dita adds butter and a sprinkle of salt to her turkish bread and then mops up the remains of her egg yolk and the slimy gleam of the bacon fat. And then?

That's it. I leave.

There was a full moon. The silver glistened and vibrated on the sea as she neared the northern end of the beach on her walk back home that night. She passed the Bondi RSL club, the Bidigal reserve and the single Bondi sandhill up on her left. There weren't many people around at that hour. Heading along Campbell Parade, it was quiet. The pub and the cafés were closed.

The surf was big, the waves crashed dramatically over the rocks, the reef and the swimming pool at the south end of the beach. In Notts Avenue, she stopped at the surf viewing area just before the baths and watched the rising swell of the ocean for a few moments. She continued along Bondi Road, walking fast up the hill, pleased the steepness doesn't faze her, not panting, managing it nice and easy, even in her high heels. She crossed at the lights near the pub on the corner.

A cold wind blew and then it began to rain.

She passed the laneway on her right and was heading for the shortcut home. She planned to cross the open car park of the block of units, and then down through the little park that leads to the hole in the fence that usually gets her home in no time. It was not until she was in the empty car park that she heard her own footsteps squelching on the wet surface and realised that there was another set of sounds behind her. Her shoes made a squench, squash noise and that's why she didn't realise at first what the other sound was – and that the sound had been there for some time.

The man has a gruff, heavily accented Australian voice, his face was masked with a dark balaclava and he wore dark-coloured tracksuit pants – the same description given by his first two victims. His threats, including that he was armed with a knife, were similar to words spoken in the first two attacks and appeared well rehearsed. After each attack, he casually walked away.

Anny veered left as she changed course and retraced her steps without turning towards the footsteps. After moving some distance away and towards the safety of the lights of the units and a door that she could bang on in case of emergency, she turned around to see if the person was still there. He was there all right. In joggers, tracksuit, medium height, average build. He'd stopped at the point where she veered left and was looking down into the empty park.

Sorry, she thought she heard him say as he looked over towards her.

She turned and hurried back towards the road and the street lights leaving him behind. She walked on the side of the road towards the oncoming traffic just like she does when she's on her solitary travels in Europe, and the man receded into the distance.

Dita's plate looks so shiny clean now after her mop-up with the Turkish bread it's as if the plate has come straight out of the dishwasher. Anny tells her that before she went out that night she'd worried that she'd feel tacky when she got home.

You would have if you'd gone against your instincts and allowed those people to talk you into doing something you didn't want to do, Dita says.

I feel bad, though, that this whole sex thing is such an issue for me when there's all the killing going on in Israel and the para Olympians in wheelchairs on the television every night.

You're not going around complaining. You're doing something about it. It's better than those singles dances. I only went to a couple but I felt like a lump of meat being looked up and down.

But I'm such a wimp, Anny says.

No, you're not. You went. You're not a wimp if you can go.

I'm a wimp when it comes to getting rid of guys. Some boring man always latches on to me and I end up leaving just to get rid of him, or some man attempts to follow me home.

Anny breathes out heavily and tells Dita that Richard was the one who'd told her about the place. You know Richard, the one I met on the internet.

You met him in a chat room?

No, not a chat room, Anny says, sensing Dita's disapproval. There are all sorts of loonies in chat rooms. No. A singles website. Richard said the women at these clubs do the choosing and there'd be lots of young men for me to pick from and plenty who'd want to give me a massage. In fact, I got so excited about the idea of me doing the choosing that I'd look at the men in the gym and sitting on the train and I'd think, would I choose you if you were there. Richard offered to come with me as my partner but why would I want to pay $120 to go as a couple when I can go for nothing. And anyway, I wouldn't want to see Richard with another woman.

It wasn't very complimentary to you that Richard offered to go with you, Dita says, a harsh satisfaction in her voice. Anny can see Dita is pleased somehow telling her this about Richard – as if Anny doesn't know it already.

Dita pouts her lips to apply a tangerine lipstick to her mouth. The lipstick matches her perfectly manicured toenails that are revealed at the end of her stiletto sandals. She puts the lipstick away in her handbag, sits back and looks out to the ocean, then twists her wedding ring around her finger.

It's a can that I've always wanted to open, Dita says. To see what goes on in these places. She stands up decisively and pulls her T-shirt down at the sides, accentuating the waistless bulge of her torso that protrudes for some distance from her body. She slides her hands up and down over her stomach like a proud pregnant woman, but Dita isn't pregnant.

She thrusts her shoulders back and her chest out. Who cares if my gut hangs out, she says proudly. I've got a gorgeous husband, two mortgages, two kids and a great business. What more could a girl want?

Anny feels depressed. But she won't tell her that. She's said enough already.

After the Games

1.

Anny saw him again today. He looked older. Their paths crossed on the cliffs between Bronte and Bondi. He walked with a woman she had never seen before. The woman had long beautiful legs – bronzed a clear nut-brown. She was wearing a man's undershirt and brown shorts and had a crochet bag hanging loosely from a black nylon strap draped over her hips. Her hair was long and it flicked out in golden corkscrews over her shoulders and down her back. They were laughing. He walked right past Anny and kept right on walking.

2.

The beach seems unusually quiet today, apart from a yoga class taking place on the grassy verge behind the pavilion. On the ocean, surfers in wetsuits loll motionless on surfboards. On the sand, a gaggle of seagulls stand rigid as Irish dancers. And over on the rocks at the southern end of the beach other seagulls laze in the early sun in groups of three or four, or six or eight – their chests puffed out, feathers bristling in the spring breeze, as they nestle into the face of the rock.

It is shortly after the Sydney 2000 Olympic Games and Anny is on a rostered day off from her job with the ABC. She is also a poet but she doesn't refer to that unless it is something people know already. She doesn't think of making a living as a poet, not only because the income would be non-existent, but because she thinks, as she has innumerable times in her life, that probably she will not write any more poems.

On the grass, a woman works out with her female personal trainer.

The trainer holds an oblong plastic cushion at waist height while the woman kicks the bag. One, two, three, calls out the trainer.

Kick, kick, kick, goes the woman's leg hard into the cushion.

Four, five, six.

Kick, kick.

That's the way, the trainer encourages. Nine, ten, she continues with a rising inflection in her voice. The trainer is forced backwards slightly with each kick but makes a quick recovery to her original position.

3.

A man and a woman lie together kissing, sheltered by the shadow of the rocks at the southern end of the beach. Anny came here at night with Howard and they sat over there near the rocks with their arms around each other into the night. The pull of the tide kept bringing the waves closer to their feet. Anny saw the froth advancing and retreating and her own toes digging into the sand. All the time he spoke, she saw her feet and when they started to go numb in the damp sand she knew without looking up what he was going to say; the whole of her seemed to be in her toes. Her love was in the waves. For some reason, she thought that if the waves reached her, things would work out between them. The waves advanced and retreated but never quite reached the rock where they sat: never quite bridged the gap, the space between them and the ocean.

4.

On the sand a one-legged seagull hops towards the water labouring over the crumbs of loose sand which break away and roll down as he passes over them. The one-legged seagull seems to have a definite goal in sight differing from the high-hopping tangerine-footed bird who attempts to cross in front of him, and who waits for a moment with his black beak trembling as if in deliberation, and then hops off as rapidly and strangely in the opposite direction. A line of seaweed with deep green lakes in the hollows lies between the seagull and the water's edge where the other gulls are pecking for food. The seagull waits, undecided whether to circumvent the mountain of seaweed or to breast it.

Anny stops and watches the struggle of the seagull.

5.

The ocean is grey and flat today. It is so quiet in fact that she can hear the tiny whisper of the breeze, the rustling of the waves approaching the shore, the creaking of the wings of a gull-like bird which flies low over the promenade and the flapping of her own thin skirt as it blows against her legs. But there is no wind, nothing but a steady pressure forward as she progresses along the beach. Somewhere behind the veil of clouds there is a pale sun which can be seen, in the far distance, that casts a white gleam on the water.

Who would know there had been a beach volleyball stadium here on the beach at Bondi? She bought tickets for the preliminaries for herself and her son. They hadn't been out, just the two of them, since he was a little boy when she took him to a Kiss concert.

After the game, they'd walked back to her place and he'd come in briefly for a glass of water before saying goodbye. She'd kissed him on the neck – on that soft groove that she used to know so well when he was a little boy.

When he'd left, she couldn't think of anything for the rest of the afternoon except that soft part of his neck and the kiss.

6.

Near the end of the promenade, a woman cradles a baby in her arms. Anny can see the baby's face clearly as it is lit by the sun. She can almost smell the baby's soft hair, that familiar baby smell she once knew. The woman strokes the baby and looks down at it and the baby looks back up at her. She looks up again with a faraway gaze that all new mothers seem to have and rocks slowly from side to side, her feet shuffling against the cement. The light picks up the woman's high cheekbones and glints off her glasses.

Anny moves to the left as a woman pushing a three-wheeled stroller runs past. The baby clutches the sides of the pram, the front wheel lifting as the woman negotiates the corner.

7.

Anny first met Howard at a dinner party at a mutual friend's house. He'd talked business with the host and she hadn't really connected with him. It was only towards the end of the meal when he'd passed her the chocolate-covered strawberries and encouraged her to eat one that she'd warmed to him slightly. Go on, he'd said. Have one. Chocolate is good for you. He was a chunky sort of a bloke, a thick head of brown hair, greying at the sides. She had to admit that she wasn't attracted to him when they first met.

You were disappointed, I could tell, he said later. A week after the dinner, he'd rung and asked her out for dinner. He'd come over to pick her up and they'd walked down to Bondi. Coming back to her place later, he told her he knew she was interested in him because she kept brushing into his arm as they walked up the hill.

8.

Anny trusts what she makes of things – usually. She trusts what she thinks about friends and chance acquaintances, but she feels stupid and helpless when contemplating the collision of herself and Howard. She has plenty to say about it, given the chance, because she likes to explain things, but she doesn't trust what she says, even to herself; it doesn't help her. Because everything and everyone else in his life came before me, she might say. His two businesses, his children, his ex-wife who lived across the road.

9.

The one-legged seagull has now considered every possible method of reaching his goal without going round the line of seaweed or climbing over it. Aside from the effort required to climb the seaweed, he is doubtful whether the slippery texture will bear his weight. This determines him finally to creep beneath it, for there is a point where the seaweed curves high enough from the ground to admit him. He inserts his head in the opening and takes stock of the high brown roof and is getting used to the cool brown light before deciding what to do next.

10.

Howard had said he uses his air rifle to kill birds. He said he's proud to shoot introduced birds around his house – and has no hesitation in killing dive-bombing magpies and noisy possums.

She remembers his house well. Big, two storeys, red-brick, four bedrooms, two bathrooms, a swimming pool out the back. Black leather and chrome, art books on the coffee tables. Huge original paintings on the walls.

He'd stay in the family room when his children were visiting, which was seven days out of fourteen – everyone in their own special seat at a computer or watching television or talking on the telephone. There was no spare seat for Anny and not enough light to read by.

She bought flowers. She bought presents for his children; clothes for the girls; she talked music with his son. She learned pathways around the house and found places outside where she could sit.

She'd felt flattered when he said that he wanted her to move in with him. He offered to build her a studio out the back. A dog house, a friend had said. He wants you out the back in the dog house so he can keep an eye on you. So you can be on hand whenever it suits him.

Howard talked about all the women his friends had lined up for him – waiting to be introduced. He spoke about a former girlfriend and how he wanted her to move in with him but she wouldn't, so he ended the relationship. Later, Anny found out that Howard had kept on seeing the former girlfriend, even ringing her from Paris from the conference Anny had foolishly agreed to attend with him. She'd stupidly insisted on paying her own business class airfare, which she couldn't afford, in order to be by his side.

She didn't know any of this until it was too late – until she'd become needy and dependent.

You just want a handbag, a doormat, a warm body in the bed, she'd accused him.

I have a fatal flaw, he'd explained. I only want what I cannot have.

And what are Anny's flaws? Angry, demanding, uncooperative Anny. Anny, the unsatisfactory poet.

11.

Two pigeons waddle along the concrete in search of food. Their tails wag back and forth, their necks jut in and out like finely linked springs moving to the rhythm of their webbed feet. On the grass, the men and women practising yoga twist their bodies into unimaginable knots and drop into breathtaking back bends, seeming to hang suspended in the air as they jump from one position to the next. The clear measured voice of the female yoga teacher calls out instructions.

Push down through the buttocks

Pull up through the ribcage

Relax the head down

Spread the fingers out wide

Toes under

Push the hips up

Keep the mind focused in the moment

Roll over on to your back

And come into the corpse position.

If you live alone and you can't close your hand, it makes life very difficult as you get older, says the yoga instructor. Not being able to open a jar or turn a key in the lock. Every morning when I wake up, I take the time to stretch out my body, she continues. I rotate my ankles, stretch out my feet and arms, and then I stand up and stretch out my neck. How many of you stretch in the mornings? Living in the city takes a toll on our health. We sit at a desk writing or sit at the computer – but we need to stretch the hands, the wrists, the hip flexors and to keep our bodies moving.

Anny wonders if the early morning stretches are only for people who live alone – for people who don't wake up with their lover beside them.

12.

The last time she saw Howard, they sat in her car near Ben Buckler in the rain. She rested her hands against the steering wheel, then leant back and listened as the windscreen started to fog. She felt the rise and the fall of her own breathing but she couldn't hear her heart or her breath. She knew without seeing that the waves were colliding. Below, the swells rolled against the brown cliffs that she couldn't see.

When she drove back to her apartment, she sat down on a chair in her bedroom. She sat for an hour or so, then went to the bathroom, undressed, put on her nightgown, and got into bed. In bed she felt relief, that she had got myself home safely and would not have to think about anything any more.

In fact, her only memory now is of the sound of the windscreen wipers swinging back and forth as she and Howard sat in silence in her car.

After the Maccabi bridge collapse in Israel, she rang to see if his daughter had been involved. She left a message on his answer machine but he never returned her call. He wrote to her care of the ABC, to say he'd pack and send her things.

13.

The grey underside of wings flap as a triangle of seagulls fly past in perfect formation above the rocks. They climb to a thousand feet, then, flapping their wings as hard as they can, they push over into a blazing steep dive toward the waves. They pull sharply upward again into a full loop and then fly all the way around to a dead-slow stand-up landing on the sand.

14.

Effortlessly the one-legged seagull spreads his wings and lifts into the air. In the light breeze, he curves his feathers to lift himself without a single flap of wing from sand to cloud and down again.

He climbs two thousand feet above the sea, and without a moment for thought of failure and death, he brings his fore wings tight in to his body, leaving only the narrow swept wingtips extended into the wind, and falls into a vertical dive.

With the faintest twist of his wingtips, he eases out of the dive and shoots above the waves, a grey cannonball under the sun.

He trembles ever so slightly with delight.

15.

She had his sweater draped over her shoulders. They were laughing. Anny watched their backs move away. She waited by the sea until the sun went down.

16.

The swell is up, the Pacific Ocean expressing its power across the rocks below Anny in spectacular explosions of spray.

It is colder now and the day is fading. A little wind has blown up. The wind tears at her hair. With a wild gesture, she pulls her hair loose from its side combs and lets it stream across her face and then lets it fly back in the wind.

A weak sun emerges. She stands still and lifts her face.

17.

Keep your hips still, swing your arms, keep your lower abdominals tight to protect your back. Try to keep your chest high, a nice long neck. Keep your arms out nice and long. Relax the shoulders. Stand tall. Go over to the right side, keep your knees soft. Very slowly. And the other side. Forward roll. Drop the chin into the neck. Hold it. Keep your knees soft and come back up. Really concentrate on spinal articulation here – vertebrae by vertebrae slowly roll it up, shoulders relaxed. Chin in, roll it down. Keep those knees soft. Bend your knees as much as you have to. Go down for four, push it in. Stretch out the shoulders there. Hold it and release the hands on to the ground and roll it back up. Take your right leg out in front. Hands on the hips, keep the hips square. We're going over in a nice square line. Should be able to stretch the hamstrings there.

And…coming back up.

It's Not Easy Being On Holidays

On the balcony

It was a sunny Friday afternoon at the holiday house, 'Santa Barbara', six kilometres from Byron Bay. The dog slept soundly on the grass under a palm tree. The mosquitoes nibbled at everyone's feet. Max lit a citronella candle and placed it under the table.

Max wasn't wearing his little white panama hat today, although his forehead was red and so were his bald patch and his nose. He wore a pink sarong decorated with white frangipanis. He told Anny he'd just had a shower and put factor 15 all over. He was waiting to go to the beach with his lover, Robert, and Anny was waiting to go with her friend, Ruby. All together in a rented Toyota.

Max liked things to be in order at 'Santa Barbara'. He was the first to collect the plates and the cups and stack them in the dishwasher. He kept the washing machine occupied most mornings. He made sure Robert always had clean clothes to wear and a dry swimming costume on the ready. Each night he'd put a bottle of water in the freezer so they'd have plenty of cold water for their day at the beach. Max and Robert worked carefully and diligently on their suntans. And each afternoon after their day at the beach Max watched over Robert as Robert worked on his bicep development by swimming fifty laps of the Olympic-sized swimming pool beside the beach. Max, being of English descent, had a fairer complexion and because he didn't swim the daily laps his body was more on the flabby side.

He collected the six empty coffee cups and took them into the kitchen. The rest of the group continued to read their books in various reclining positions around the table. The dull hum of cicadas in the background.

Max returned with a bottle of cold water from the fridge and picked up the dry costumes hanging over the wooden rail of the balcony. Are we bulldogs or Speedos today? he asked Robert.

Speedos, said Robert, who was lounging on a cane chair with his feet up on the pine coffee table.

Max began to pack for their day at the beach. He placed the swimming costumes and the bottle of water into his backpack with beach towels and suntan lotion.

Anny watched him as he arranged the objects in his pack. The towels neatly folded, the water bottle wrapped in plastic.

I'm so busy on the beach, he said to Anny. Pamela sits and talks to me. Robert goes for a walk. I'm up and down to the water – that sort of thing. He sighed.

Anny nodded with understanding. It's not easy being on holidays, she said.

Max adjusted the knot on his sarong, pulling the frangipani pattern together at his waist so the material clung tightly to his hips.

I can see you're not wearing much today, she said. Only a sarong!

It's very cool like this, said Max.

Anny said, On New Year's Eve I ran my hand up the inside of a man's trousers from the ankles up and discovered he wasn't wearing any underwear either.

You discovered a little something?

A big something, she said.

They both laughed.

It was a year ago that Ruby invited Anny to join her on the holiday. They'd been out walking on a Saturday morning as they usually did at weekends, that is, before Ruby met her new boyfriend, David. Ruby said she'd also be inviting her friend, Annabel, and another friend, Robert.

Anny had known Robert when they were teenagers but hadn't seen him again until they met up at Ruby's birthday party, six months ago. He was at the party with his lover, Max. At the party, Robert had reminisced about visiting Anny when they were teenagers. He remembered sitting in the window box in her parents' house in Bellevue Hill. She'd warmed to him as they chatted about old times as Jewish teenagers growing up in the eastern suburbs of Sydney. Anny knew Robert had left his wife and children for another man causing scandal within the community and wondered what he was up to these days.

At the same party, Anny met Annabel and her lover, Pamela. That's when Anny found out that Pamela was coming on the holiday too and bringing her dog.

You don't have any objections to me bringing my dog, do you? Pamela had asked.

What could Anny say? The fact was she didn't like dogs much but found it difficult to tell a dog lover that she didn't fancy her dog.

On the balcony with Max

'Santa Barbara' was a wooden bungalow set up a gravel driveway surrounded by gums and palms and ferns – green and lush. It nestled in a rainforest-like oasis with another house beside it. The two houses shared a driveway. Apart from the trees in the backyard, the only other things to be seen from the balcony were a big black garbage bin on wheels, a clothesline, a compost heap and the curve of the road behind.

In the kitchen, Ruby was sweeping the wooden floor, as she did each day after each meal. The sunlight lit up the kitchen, showing up her short-cropped woolly hair against her pale face. Her wide hips and solid thighs were hidden under a long loose T-shirt and black knee-length tights.

As usual, she had an opera playing on the stereo as she worked. Today it was *La Traviata* – over and over as she emptied the dish-washer, scrubbed down all the bench tops, sorted out the rubbish for recycling, swept the floor.

Outside on the balcony sat Max and Anny, Robert and Annabel. Max was bent over the coffee table writing a postcard. Anny was doing her best to read a book, but the uncomfortable straight-backed dining chair made it difficult to concentrate. Robert and Annabel read their books on the two comfortable cane lounge chairs. They'd got in first.

Through the window, Anny watched Ruby sweeping. Ruby finished cleaning the kitchen and then went upstairs to ring up. She rang home every day. First her mother, then her daughter and then her new boyfriend, David. The problem was that she rang from the bedroom that she shared with Anny. Always the door was closed during these long conversations and Anny couldn't get into the room.

Anny lay her book face down on the table and stood up. Anyone for a tea or coffee? she asked.

Not for me, said Robert.

No thanks, said Annabel.

I'll have a coffee, said Max.

Full cream, light white, skim milk, full cream soy or light soy? asked Anny.

Normal thanks. Black.

What are you writing on the postcard?

Having a wonderful time with Robert, wish you were here. That sort of thing. And, all the others are into daily exercise and eating carrots and lettuce. There are so many vegetables there's hardly room for my slab in the fridge.

Anny laughed, realising she wasn't the only one feeling like an outsider.

On the balcony with Annabel

Annabel sat on a cane chair eating her breakfast from a bowl in her lap. As she lifted the first spoonful of muesli to her mouth, her thick gold necklace sparkled in the sun, her white lace nightie transparent in the morning light, a gold bracelet on her right hand a silver bracelet on her left, diamond earrings circled with gold. Her hair streaked blonde, one strand falling on her forehead like cupid's arrow through her heart-shaped face. Anny complimented Annabel on the beauty and variety of her necklaces.

I brought all my jewellery with me because I've been robbed three times in Balmain, Annabel explained.

Anny wondered about the security of the bungalow – set back from the street with sliding glass doors from floor to ceiling covered by fly screens.

This house isn't exactly secure.

That's why I keep all my jewellery with me in my handbag.

In your handbag!

Anny sipped her coffee and watched a power walker stride down the road, white joggers flashing, as a boy bicycled up the hill. I'm surprised you haven't spent more time with Ruby on this holiday, she said. I thought you were such close friends. And that you'd want to do things together.

Annabel adjusted her position in the chair and breathed in deeply. From the first day we got here, she's treated me as if I'm invisible, said Annabel. She looks straight through me.

Why would she do that?

Annabel lit up a cigarette. She's like that, she said. Ruby hated my last girlfriend. And my girlfriend hated her. It was a real problem. I could only see Ruby by myself. I think Ruby's always had a crush on me but I don't feel the same way about her.

I'm upset with Ruby too, said Anny. Once she met David, I was dropped and I didn't hear a word from her: Christmas, New Year. Nothing.

Did you say anything to her?

Yesterday I told her I missed our walks and talks. She said, 'Well, you've got me now.' And that's all. Apart from calling me a passive aggressive.

Technical talk. Us psychologists talk like that. Don't worry about it.

When she invited me on the holiday, I said I wanted my own

room. Not only haven't I got my own room but she expected me to share the double bed with her.

You don't feel comfortable about that?

No way. So we divided the mattress in half and I sleep on the floor.

Anny on the phone to her son

There's so much tension here. The girls are fighting. Pamela and Annabel are splitting up. Annabel's asked Pamela to move out when they go back home. I don't know why they both came on this holiday.

Are they fighting with you too?

No, I stay out of it. Not much of a holiday, though. Everyone is into booze and smoking and getting stoned every night.

How old are these people?

My age.

What about Ruby? Aren't you doing things with her?

She's dieting and exercising like a loony. She's no fun to be with. Only eats a lettuce leaf if we go out and she's on the phone to David every day.

And the dog? You were worried about the dog.

Surprisingly, he's very docile. Makes me wonder, I mean Pamela being a policewoman. And the bloody hire car is a manual, which means I can't drive it.

Come home if you're having an awful time.

Another night in Byron

On Wednesday night, Max and Robert, Ruby and Anny drove up towards the house. The headlights lit up the driveway as they negotiated the curve between the houses. Ruby drove, Robert sat next to her, and Max and Anny sat in the back. Max and Anny shared a joke about the bloke who lived in the house on the right-hand side up the same driveway. They often caught him outside on his balcony in his white cotton underpants when they drove in towards his front door to turn around. Max and Anny both looked forward to this moment when they'd turn in and be able to put him in the spotlight sitting in his underwear on his steps having a beer. Ruby always reversed in the wrong way and got stuck on the pebbles, so Max and Anny had plenty of time to look out for their man, to see where they'd caught him and in what state of undress.

After much noisy gravel grating and spinning of wheels, Ruby manoeuvred into their parking area under the house. They hauled the plastic shopping bags out of the boot and up the steps and into the kitchen. They unpacked the food. Mangoes, bananas, grapes, chicken legs for dinner, another bag of rice, a twenty-kilo pack of carrots.

Annabel and Pamela volunteered to cook so the rest of them waited outside around the wooden table on the balcony. Everyone except Anny lit up their various kinds of cigarettes and settled back. Anny was too hungry to relax. It's bloody nine o'clock and I'm starving, she thought as she watched through the kitchen window. I need to eat on a regular basis. I feel such a pig if I go into the kitchen and help myself to food in front of everyone when no one else seems to eat much – and I don't want to prepare food for five other people.

The fluorescent light highlighted Pamela and Annabel. No cooking was happening yet. They were into each other instead.

Annabel lay her head on Pamela's shoulder as Pamela moved in closer and stroked Annabel's cheek. She lingered down the side of her neck, down over the thick circles of her necklace and down in between the vee of her T-shirt. Annabel reached up to Pamela's face and pulled her down lower until they were kissing again but this time more urgently – tongues probing and penetrating.

Anny turned away and looked over towards the others. But they stared out blankly into the black of the backyard too stoned to notice or to care.

Preparing the dinner with Max

Max set the table and Anny cooked the rice. Max placed the chairs from the balcony around the dining table. He gathered a cushion for each chair from the lounge then stepped back to admire the table. He looked over to Anny and grinned. I've seen more fannies than all of you put together, he said.

Anny knew Max was a male nurse, but she wondered why he'd say something like that.

The thing is, Max said, I keep thinking about Pamela and Annabel and I keep wondering – what do lesbians do?

Anny put the spoon down from stirring the rice that was sticking to the bottom of the saucepan. I don't know. Why?

Well, said Max, Pamela said that Annabel doesn't want to have sex with her any more. She said they're breaking up when they go back, so best to not have sex on the holiday. She said, 'What am I supposed to do? Annabel lies there with her legs wide open. What does she expect me to do?'

Anny continued to dig at the rice.

Max walked over to the CD player and sifted through the cassettes. A click, and then the thud of house music. Max waved his arms in the air, puffed his chest out, shoulders back, swayed his hips. Anny couldn't help herself – she had to move to the beat. She and Max danced to the same rhythm connected by the archway to the kitchen.

Turn that music down! Ruby called out from upstairs. Isn't there any classical music?

Max and Anny smirked at each other.

Do you remember that dreadful opera she kept playing over and over when we first arrived? he said.

Anny raised her eyebrows towards the ceiling and they kept dancing.

Ruby and Anny

A small table separated Ruby's bed and Anny's mattress on the floor. On the table were a bedside light and the telephone. Sliding screen doors led out to a balcony that was directly above the downstairs balcony.

Ruby turned sideways to the full-length floor mirror. She patted and rubbed her stomach flat as she turned from one side to the other admiring her body. She'd stopped eating as far as Anny could see. Max thought her face looked dreadful. Haggard is how he described it to Anny. But then Ruby thinks Max is a bitch. The Queen Bitch is what she said.

Anny waited for Ruby to finish so she could get up. There was only room for one person to be standing at any one time. She put her book down on her half of the bedside table and looked up at Ruby. I wish I had my own room, she said. If I did meet a bloke, I'd have nowhere to bring him, she added, half complaining, half joking in her tone.

You'd just have to go back to his place.

As if I'd go back to some blokes place I'd just met, and anyway I can't drive the car.

Ruby continued her toilette at the dressing table. Eyeshadow, eyeliner, mascara, lipstick.

Anny looked out the glass doors to the splayed pine fronds. He's a nice bloke Robert, said Anny. I like the way he speaks and thinks. He's articulate and logical. Interesting to listen to.

He is a solicitor! said Ruby, as if that would explain everything. He swings both ways you know. A note of confidentiality in her voice.

But he prefers men?

He did have a one-year relationship with a woman a couple of years ago.

Anny couldn't help thinking that she had so much in common with Robert. He seemed to understand her – like last night re the salad. They both wanted a crisp, light, palate cleanser. Not Ruby's heavy soggy salad with added pine and macadamia nuts.

There'd been much discussion around the dinner table. Dressing or no dressing – French style, Italian, mayonnaise – what brand of mayonnaise. A refreshing mixture of green leaves only or added tomato, capsicum, avocado – or even Greek style with feta and black olives. Or what about raw onions to give it a kick? Ruby had taken it to heart that they didn't like her salad and resolved not to make another one.

Time spent alone with Robert

Robert rested. He read a book stretched out along the length of the lounge, his bare feet hanging over the end. Anny stood on her head in a yoga pose on the carpet.

Anny on the phone to her son

We go shopping for food to Woollies every day and cook for six people every night.

That's not my idea of a holiday. Can't they afford to eat out?

They want to cook. Even on the first day when we arrived at Ballina airport, we did the supermarket shopping and all squashed in the rented car – shopping bags, suitcases and all.

If that were me, that's when I would have got back on the plane and gone straight back home.

And Pamela and Annabel all over each other in front of me. I can't stand it.

Would it worry you so much if they were straight?

I can't stand anyone being passionate in front of me – straight or gay. It makes me jealous. It's so inconsiderate of them.

Well, what did you expect going on a holiday with two gays, two lesbians, a bisexual and a dog?

You're right.

Waiting for the bathroom

Anny waited for Ruby to come out of the bathroom. She'd been in there for hours.

Inconsiderate selfish bitch, thought Anny. It would be nice to get into the fucking bathroom.

She's still in there.

Waiting to get a lift into town

Grey sky, humid, damp upper lip, the low buzz of cicadas. Ruby and Anny and Robert sat on the balcony.

How much did I spend yesterday? said Ruby to herself.

What? said Robert and Anny in unison.

I'm just working out how much I spent yesterday, said Ruby.

Who gives a shit? thought Anny.

Max brushed his teeth in the laundry. One of the lesbians was in the bathroom. That's how Max and Anny talked about them to each other – the lesbians.

Waiting for a lift with Max

Pamela yelled out from the kitchen.

Who's eaten all the mangoes? – in that angry voice of hers that they now knew so well.

Max and Anny were sitting on the balcony waiting for a lift into town.

Pamela stormed out through the kitchen door towards them. She shouted at Max first. How many did you have?

Max rested his cigarette in the ashtray before answering. Robert and I shared one with our dessert last night.

Pamela turned to Anny with her hands on her hips. And how many did you have?

Anny took another sip of her tea. Half a mango yesterday and half today, she said, unable to keep a note of apology out of her voice.

Pamela stamped her foot. I haven't had one the whole holiday, she yelled out to the trees.

Max sighed and rescued his cigarette from the ashtray. He dragged in deeply. Anny turned her attention to her tea cup, then stood up and walked quickly into the house. She climbed the wooden steps towards the bedrooms. The room she shared with Ruby was empty. Ruby's bed perfectly tucked and shaped. Anny's mattress on the floor in disarray.

She slipped into the room furtively, reminding herself it was her room as well. She put her cup of tea down beside the phone, then closed the door.

On the phone

The problem is I feel trapped. It's too far to walk into town There isn't even anywhere I can sit comfortably and read my book. There's no privacy, the chairs are dreadful, the lighting is bad in the lounge room for reading, there are mosquitoes on the balcony and the only place I can relax is in the bedroom. But half the time Ruby is in here and I can't even get into the room.

Well, come home then.

I rang the airline. But we're on some special economy ticket where you can't change the date.

Don't worry, Mum. You'll work it out.

Mandala Café

All food
Washed
And cooked
In purified
Water

At the Mandala Café

Success at last. While they were all back at the house getting stoned, Anny found a place to escape to within walking distance. Somewhere to hang out away from those loonies. They scored on the beach today so there wouldn't be any conversation tonight. Another monotonous night in Byron to look forward to, listening to the mating call of mosquitoes.

A black and white dog sniffed around the tables and nuzzled at the green and white checked tablecloths.

I'd like a cappuccino first and then a bruschetta with olive pâté, said Anny to the cute Italian guy with a ponytail. She noticed a packet of Marlboros in his pocket and an apricot stone heart around his neck on a black leather thong. She wondered where he lived – could be nearby, walking distance even.

A man with hair too blond for his dark-tanned skin and a tattooed arm puffed on a cigarette at the next table – his sleeveless T-shirt exposing his taut arms.

A well-dressed grey-haired woman sitting opposite caught Anny's eye. The woman and Anny had shared a moment of impatience earlier when they'd both waited to be served. The woman pulled a face at Anny and pointed to the flat froth on her cappuccino. The milk dipped in the middle and fell below the lip of the cup. Obviously not the standard of coffee she was used to.

Anny nodded at her with understanding and sipped the lukewarm coffee. She looked across to a park where a boy played with a dog and a frisbee.

The woman opposite pressed urgently at the buttons of a mobile phone in her hand. She frowned and looked over to Anny. Do you know how to use these things? she said in a refined English voice.

No, sorry, I don't, said Anny. I don't use them. I hate the things.

The woman pushed again at the buttons. It says PUK and enter. She jabbed again at the phone in her hand.

Sorry, I can't help you, said Anny.

I thought I was ready to cope with the things, said the woman in a shaky-with-age voice. She pursed her lips. I'll see if I can find the expert who'll tell me what to do. She drank the rest of her coffee quickly – it was obviously as cold as Anny's – then tucked her black leather envelope-shaped handbag under her arm and left.

Anny looked up at the sky. It looked like rain.

Disturbance

The phone rang as they waited on the balcony for dinner. It was Luke, the son of some friend of Ruby's. He'd called to see if he could come and stay with them at the holiday house. He'd just returned to Byron from the Woodford Festival.

I'm broke and I've got two friends with me, he said.

Ruby put him on hold and asked everyone what they thought.

No, said Anny. I don't want three extra people in the house.

It's okay by me, said Robert.

Sure, said Pamela.

I suppose so, shrugged Annabel.

So that night Luke and his mates arrived while the six of them, Max and Robert, Annabel and Pamela, Ruby and Anny, were eating dinner and it was all a bit uncomfortable. What were they meant to do? Give them the food off their plates?

Luke's long brown matted dreadlocks hung down to his thin shoulders. His new friends, who he'd met at Woodford, were brother and sister. The girl's pretty face was scattered with pink eruptions – her brother handsome in a spiky arrogant sort of a way. Ruby showed them into the kitchen and told them to help themselves. She gave them blankets and pillows off the beds and they camped down in the lounge room.

Next morning, Ruby and Anny got up early to exercise. They climbed quietly over the sleeping bodies on the floor and out the front door.

I'm very unhappy about having Luke and his friends staying, said Anny. All these people and only one bathroom.

You feel put upon having extra people in the house? Ruby stated as if reflecting back to Anny what she'd just said would make everything okay.

Anny walked on in silence.

Ruby and Anny expected everyone to be asleep when they returned to the house but the lounge room was empty and the others were gathered on the balcony obviously waiting for their return.

Pamela stood, her back against the wooden rails – her men's shorts rolled up on her thighs, a chesty Bond singlet covering her lean body, her triceps well defined. She was the first one to speak. So, you're back.

What's the problem? said Ruby.

What do you think? Pamela said, her voice louder. You walk out of here leaving us with a house full of druggies.

What are you talking about? We went for a walk.

You left us here in the house – with them!

So?

We couldn't go anywhere.

Why not?

We couldn't leave them alone in the house.

I would have thought it was obvious we were coming back. So where are they?

They're gone. We told them to get out.

You what? said Ruby, standing with both hands on her hips.

Serves you bloody well right, Ruby, thought Anny.

Last night we decided we wanted them out of here by nine. When you weren't here, we told them to go.

She told them to fuck off, said Max from the corner.

Ungrateful little bastards, said Pamela. Not a word of thanks. They didn't even say thank you.

You spoke to them like that? You told them to fuck off?

They need to be taught a lesson – you can't spend your life bludging off other people.

The veins in Ruby's neck enlarged and pulsated.

You went out, Pamela continued. You didn't tell anyone where you were going, when you'd be back.

I go for a walk every morning. I was coming back.

Don't you think you've got some responsibility here? Leaving us with Luke and his friends.

Ruby's voice came out low and moderated. You're a bunch of hypocrites, she said. You smoke and drink and get stoned. You've all had bad trips. Have you forgotten?

Annabel sat, arms folded, one leg crossed tightly across the other. You treat this house as your own, she said to Ruby. There are six of us here and we'd like to be involved in the decisions.

Ruby glanced around the group. I asked you all last night, she said.

We had to say yes because we're friends of yours, but we didn't want them staying longer than one night. We haven't been in the house for long. It should have been a night when we were bonding.

Annabel leant forward toward Ruby, grasping the sides of the chair. There was no consultation about this holiday either, she said. You invited me to come along and I thought it was just going to be you and me.

Ruby looked away. You didn't say yes straight away, she said as if speaking to the trees.

And when you invited me, I said I wanted my own room, said Anny.

I was the last one to be invited, said Max, apology in his tone.

I asked you to give me until the end of the week, said Annabel, her voice breaking up. Because you've come to this house before, you treat it like your own home and we're the guests – but we're not – we've all paid for this holiday. Annabel's hand shook as she reached for her cigarette packet. I was really looking forward to a break, she said. I so desperately needed to get away.

Ruby studied the floor on the other side of the balcony.

The fighting continues

Anny sat upstairs on the balcony outside the bedroom. She could hear the fight going on between Pamela and Ruby on the balcony beneath her. The juicer whirred in the kitchen.

Ruby shouted above the noise. Whose clothes are these in the laundry sink? They've been soaking for two days.

They've been there for one day, said Pamela, turning off the juicer.

They were there yesterday morning, said Ruby.

Don't raise your voice at me.

I'm not.

Ruby, you said, 'What are these clothes doing' in a rude tone of voice.

I asked whose clothes were soaking, said Ruby.

Ruby, you raised your voice at me.

Ruby banged the screen door.

They're at it again

Anny couldn't hear exactly what was going on downstairs but they were looking at a map of Byron Bay and Pamela and Ruby were arguing about the quickest route to Brunswick Heads. They'd planned to meet up there for a group dinner that night.

Ruby walked into the room behind Anny and closed the bedroom door.

What happened? asked Anny.

That woman's impossible. Ruby grabbed a pair of shorts and a shirt hanging on the side of the mirror and moved towards the door. Pamela's got a serious problem, said Ruby on her way out of the room.

Anny heard the bath filling up so she went downstairs to see what had been going on.

Max and Robert were on the balcony.

Max turned to Anny. Ruby stormed out after telling Pamela to 'fuck off', he said. Tsk. Tsk, he clicked his tongue and shook his head. Such language!

Annabel went upstairs to talk to Ruby in the bathroom. She perched on the side of the bath for an intimate conversation. Robert, Max and Anny stayed on the balcony while Pamela took the dog for a walk.

I've never seen Ruby behave like this before, said Robert. I'm surprised to see her flying off the handle.

Girls will be girls, said Max with a chuckle.

Later, Anny went back up to the bedroom. Ruby and Annabel sat on the bed in silence looking very serious.

I've booked a flight back to Sydney for tomorrow, said Ruby.

It's the best thing to do, said Annabel before Anny could say anything.

I'm not having any fun, explained Ruby.

Annabel walked out of the room and Anny was left with Ruby.

I'm going to put a rinse in my hair and give myself a pedicure this afternoon, said Ruby, smiling. I've rung David and he's meeting me at the airport. She said this in a conspiratorial sort of a way – pleased with herself, as if she thought Anny would be happy for her too. It's the best thing for me to do, she continued. To go back early.

Anny nodded. Only one more night with Ruby and then she'd have the room to herself.

At the carnival at Brunswick Heads

That night the six of them, Max and Robert, Pamela and Annabel, and Ruby and Anny, met up at Brunswick Heads for dinner. They ate fish and chips at the pub and then watched the woodchopping.

Anny got into an arm wrestle with the computer and then tested her strength with a punching bag. She'd taught her son to arm wrestle. They'd lie on their stomachs facing each other with their elbows touching. She showed him how to wait, to psych himself up, to feel the strain before showing his strength, to wait for the first move. At the carnival, Anny felt the muscles working in her shoulders as she rammed into the punching bag. The girls were surprised to see her boxing and gathered around, shouting encouragement. She bounced on her toes, right, right, hook with the left, smash into the leather, her rings jamming into her knuckles, bounce bounce, back in with the right, follow up with the left, left, left, hit with the left, in with the right again.

What's his name? encouraged Pamela from the sidelines. That's the way. Hit the bastard.

Goodbye Ruby

No goodbye from Ruby. They were all asleep when Ruby let herself out the front door in the morning to catch the airport bus to Ballina.

Waiting for the washing

Anny waited for Max's load of washing to finish so she could get a lift into town with the boys. He's going to take forever. By the time he hangs the washing out and finds matching pegs for each item, I'll never get out of the house.

When Max came in from the clothesline with the plastic washing basket under his arm, he looked at Anny and rolled his eyes. Matron has gone, is the way he put it.

A night on the town with Robert and Max

Max said to Anny she should pop a guarana before they went out. It will give you a natural high, he said.

I suppose. Seeing it's from the health food store. It can't be too bad.

You might meet a handsome muscly backpacker tonight, said Max.

We might meet three muscly backpackers tonight, said Anny, and they both laughed.

The three of them went to the Railway Bar after dinner. Anny and Max and Robert.

Powerful thighs, said Max looking at the guy in the denim vest astride the bench.

Robert and Anny checked him out.

Looks like head down, bum up, facing the mirror type to me, said Max.

Anny tried hard to imagine the scenario but the only way she could visualise Max bending down was to see him in a hospital ward lifting a patient carefully by the shoulders, his bald patch reflected in the mirror behind the bed.

Let's go to the beach, said Robert.

They finished their vodkas and walked out into the night. In a deserted laneway, they shared a joint and then headed for the beach. They sat back near the dunes and watched the nude bodies playing on the edge of the water, silhouetted by the sea.

Anny stretched out on the sand between the two blokes and looked up at the sky. The moon emerged from behind a dark cloud, a silver sheen reflecting down upon the ocean.

On the nude beach

Hot again. Annabel took a coach to the Gold Coast to spend some money at the casino. That left Max and Robert, Pamela and Anny. They decided to go to the nude beach. Pamela brought her dog. They took the two cars – Pamela's station wagon and Max and Robert in the rented Nissan. Pamela said she might want to come back early, so Anny went in Pamela's car because she thought she might want to come back early too – a whole day in the sun might be too much for her fair skin. She sat beside Pamela with the dog in the back. The dog leaned over the front seat with his slippery tongue hanging out in Anny's direction as they drove south along the coast.

Scattered on the beach were about a dozen or so men reclining in the sun. Anny undressed quickly, ran down to the water and dived into the cool, cool water. Max and Robert paddled around in the shallows. Pamela threw a stick to her dog by the water's edge.

Later, Anny lay back in the shade under the trees. She stretched out with a sigh, her hands and feet scrunching into the tender sand. Max and Robert and Pamela lay face up in the sun nearby.

I hope Pamela doesn't think I'm trying to crack on to her, thought Anny, closing her legs.

A man walked up towards them and then behind them and back across the sand.

He's on the hunt, said Robert.

In the distance, a small motorboat approached the shore. As the boat neared, Anny noticed the driver of the boat was naked as he stood up to manoeuvre the boat into shore. On either side of him were large iceboxes of ice creams for sale. He heaved the boat onto the sand and Anny couldn't help but notice the red imprints on his bottom from his sitting position in the boat.

Gradually the men on the beach sauntered towards the boat with money clasped in their bare hands. They lined up one behind the other as they waited their turn, assorted body shapes and colours. Tight firm bums, droopy wrinkly bums. Some with telltale underwear marks and others browned all over.

Do you want an icecream? asked Max.

Why don't we have lunch now instead, said Robert.

Max unpacked the esky on to a towel over on a grassy patch. Bread, crackers, cheese, chicken liver pâté, grapes, apples. red wine. He beckoned to Anny. She wrapped a sarong around herself and sat beside them on their joined towels. Max opened the red wine and arranged the food. He cored the apples and cut them into quarters

Pamela declined an invitation to join in the picnic lunch and joined the ice cream queue instead. Her dog ran up towards the trees and barked at movement in the scrubby hiding place.

Who knows what goes on in those bushes, said Max.

Robert helped himself to some pâté and spread it with a knife on a salt biscuit. The biscuit broke as he pressed down with the knife and the crumbs fell into his pubic hair. He brushed the crumbs away.

Max leant back on his elbows nibbling on a bunch of grapes. He knocked the bottle of red wine beside him. The bright red liquid seeped into the white sand.

A fly buzzed around the apples.

A trail of ants marched towards the bread.

The Brie softened in the sun.

JM

I've never told anyone. To think about it makes my hands sweat and nausea rise from my stomach. It happened the year I turned eighteen on a sunny late afternoon in February, on the top floor of a building in Double Bay. I was recently engaged to be married and the wedding was booked for the end of June. We had gone to the photographer's studio to have our engagement photos taken. The photographer was a good friend of my future brother-in-law. I had met him several times before and had thought of him as old, as my parents seemed to be old, but he can't in those days have been more than fifty. He was tiny like a jockey, his trademark cravat tied at the neck beneath a tailored shirt. His accent, foreign but very English. His shirt covered the numbers branded on his arm – a childhood survivor of the holocaust.

I remember his navy and white cravat tied at the throat, but have to imagine his small white hands as he poured vodka into liqueur glasses and the smile he must have worn on his face, encouraging me to watch the development process in the dark room after my fiancé went back to work.

Looking back at that afternoon, I see myself as an ignorant half-adolescent, half-woman, shy, dreamy and vulnerable, in a rush to be grown-up and living away from my parents. I longed for marriage to set me free.

I remember the way he held his fingers when he sipped from the vodka, as if drinking from a delicate china cup. He had challenged me. Said, 'You're a woman now, aren't you?'

I have lost touch with that person I used to be at eighteen, with what it felt like to be about to be married to a man who I loved more than he loved me.

It is almost spring. I am walking through the gully of a park near where I live, from one end to the other. Walking is a form of relaxation, in which the legs take over. They go their own way. I watch the ground, all the way there and back, take stock of the sounds and smells, and the physical transformations, when I feel my shoulders return to their sockets as I wander along the path by the creek and through the trees.

During the period of our engagement, I was being checked out by my future brother-in-law re my suitability to marry his wife's brother. It was a reminder that I needed to show I could fit in to a European lifestyle: home-baked gugelhupf and bishops bread, veal schnitzel, thinly sliced cucumbers soaked in vinegar and sugar, hot milk for the coffee served in a ceramic jug, Persian rugs on wooden floors.

I had emerged from dumpy adolescence into tiny-waisted, exciting womanhood. By spending whole afternoons in front of the bedroom mirror and catching my reflection in shop windows, and from the attention of some of the boys at the Saturday night dances, I discovered I had changed, from a large adolescent into a petite woman. I had brown curly hair like my aunt and my skin burnt and freckled in the sun before turning a honey-gold.

My father had seemed surprised that a mature man with his own successful business and good financial prospects began to visit our house. 'Is he married already?' he asked, his eyebrows in a scowl above his newspaper.

He was shocked, now that he saw me through a man's eyes, at how far I had come from the young girl I was, my hair wound into curls like Shirley Temple by my mother's home-perm kit, wearing frilly dresses he brought back from America from his business trips. If only my mother had been stricter with me, this older man wanting to marry me would never have happened. It was all my mother's fault for letting me grow up too quickly, like letting me buy that strapless dress for the school dance. 'You want to attract attention from boys,' he accused me from across the breakfast table.

The fact is, I had exceeded, almost beyond my own expectations, in making myself look older. My mother must have wondered at times if I could ever be toned down with my body-hugging dresses, my geometric-cut hair with its dark rinse (wanting to look like Elizabeth Taylor), the black kohl pencil around the eyes, the eyeshadow, the stick-on false eyelashes, the thick foundation applied with a wet sponge. Not that this helped the outbreaks of pimples. I was out of their control and the pimples were out of my control. My mother was proud that I was getting married. When my father complained, she shook her head and dismissed him.

This is one of the places where I like to go, this park that is a creek valley with trees, shrubs and grasses growing on the sides of the basin and a watercourse where lizards and frogs laze. Twelve hectares of urban bush land not far from where I live.

I enjoy walking along the winding network of paths, down through the bush vegetation that link a series of gazebos, bridges and staircases. On the sides of the lower valley, where the tennis courts are, rainforest plants of blueberry ash, lilly-pilly and black wattle reflect the afternoon light.

I stop at a café near the courts, where lilac wisteria drapes the white painted wooden posts of the veranda. The branches of the wisteria are twisted around its own trunk. The sound of the punch of a tennis ball between two women on the court. In the café are cane high-backed chairs around small square tables. A group of white-clad tennis ladies stands up to leave. On the table are their water glasses beside screwed-up white paper serviettes and an empty water jug. When they depart, the glasses, the serviettes and the jug are the only sign that they have visited this place.

I am back in the photographic studio on that summer afternoon.

He unlocked the darkroom, rested his shoulder against the door and motioned me into the room. It was heavy with the smell of chemicals. I walked towards the tanks where the film lay and then moved around the edge of the baths. I was surrounded by darkness.

'Ah,' he said, sighing. 'This is where it all happens.'

The room was appearing through the dark as my eyes became accustomed to the shadows. The black-clad windows, hanging trapped in the dark, kept out the outside streets, where people were doing their shopping or drinking short blacks at the sidewalk cafés or driving around looking for somewhere to park in the congested streets.

He pointed to one of the tanks and I moved over to look. 'There,' he said, 'that's the film in developing agent.' He handed me my glass and moved around beside me. 'What you can see is the first step of processing – can you see?'

I looked. It was remarkable. Later it was the pre-soaking, the dilution of the developer, submerging of the film, the timer, the push-cap on the tank, the ringing of the timer. The magic of developing photographs.

'I still feel euphoric when working in the darkroom,' he said.

Why didn't I say something? His body rubbing against mine, his hands, his lips. What are you doing?

I watched. It was miraculous. The pre-soaking, the dilution of the developer, the submerging of the film, the click of the push-cap on the tank… and then the ringing of the timer. The stop bath, the fixer, the film exposed to light, the wetting agent, submerging the reel.

'You hang it up for drying for four to eight hours so it has enough time to dry and harden,' he said.

I wasn't used to alcohol, especially spirits. It immobilised me. My back pushed against a tank. I was overwhelmed, felt no power to control the moves. But I must have known what was going on.

He came very quickly.

My eyes were blurred with tears as I searched for my handbag in the reception area. I did not turn and face him, did not say anything, agreeing in my youthful ignorance, in a silence that was as good as a handshake, to carry the weight of this secret. With my high heels clicking on the concrete I walked unsteadily down the narrow passageway of the stairs that led out to the street and out into the daylight of the life that lay ahead.

The sound of water flowing over rocks in the creek hides lizards and tadpoles in the park. Smooth-barked apple, eucalyptus and tick bush on the sandy slopes. A blue-tongue lizard backs away as I pass, his chubby-splayed feet clutching at the path. Another lizard darts to safety, his body curling and curving into escape.

A small cement truck grinds down the cobbled pathway by the tennis courts. It tips cement into the mould for a wheelchair access ramp to the café. So many men to make a simple ramp – one carrying a wooden plank, one tapping at the wooden structure, two others in fluorescent vests who watch, instruct and chat. Their hair is spiked and hatless in the sun. Dark glasses wrap their browned faces.

'I married you because you were suitable,' my husband said. 'I wasn't wearing rose-coloured glasses.'

It all comes back.

All these years later, it is difficult to see the point in being back there, to be that ignorant, vulnerable eighteen-year-old girl I used to be.

The orange revolving light on top of the small concrete truck flashes. I look around at the tiny buds of spring that are framed by sticky spider webs. The webs don't loosen their grip in the breeze.

The frangipani tree is devoid of foliage or flowers. But spring is on its way. The afternoon light on the tips of the green leaves on the terraced sides and layered rock shelves, barely move in the soft breeze.

Is this the end of one thing and the beginning of another? Will all that is familiar change into something else? Walking home, I have no sense that anything has happened, that a shift may have taken place. Was it something in myself that has been waiting for so long and was finally brought to consciousness, that triggered something in me? Is it seeing the park poised to burst into spring, or watching the transformation of cement into a bridge connecting the cobbled path to the wooden veranda that make me realise that nothing is final or beyond change?

The Backpack

What can a man who meets you at the station and offers to carry your backpack mean to a woman travelling the world alone?

I was scared, like anyone who has no sense of direction. The journey was a series of stops and starts. Whether to use the Eurail pass or post it back home and ask the kids to get me a refund.

Giovanni appeared one European winter, thick padded jacket, woollen beanie, scarf and gloves, tall and imposing, I'll carry your bag.

I was small, the backpack the length of my spine, the zip-off bag on one shoulder, the daypack positioned in front like a nine-month baby bump.

That evening, as we climbed the steps of the Corniche – the wind bitter across the Mediterranean, the metal stairs covered with slippery ice, the railing melting beneath my hand. Soon it would become my railway platform, my steps, and Giovanni my landlord.

We walked there in the crisp night air. My own place. It didn't cost much. No one yet knew I was here. I could ask Giovanni if I needed any help. I knew my children would be pleased I had a base. I didn't want them to worry. It was the thing I wanted the most secretly, studying maps, absorbing travel books. To be safe, a desire whispered to the moon that moved behind my shoulder at night. If you guide me to a safe haven, I promise to be happy. And the moon listened. I did my best.

The winter sky closed down and the spring began its flowering. I took photos and painted and rang the children every week. Watch your money, don't talk to strangers, be careful walking at night – you know the drill. The pebbly beach, the weekend markets, it was all there for the exploring. A glimpse of the sea between terracotta roofs – a vision in turquoise. The cobbled streets could show which way to follow – and none of them wrong. A room at the top of the stairs – till June I stayed reading the English books Giovanni had left in the bookcase, shopping for food, telling my kids and friends they should come for a visit.

Where had the months gone? Almost two years on the road. Summer approached. The rents would go up and the tourists arrive. Time to move on. I could only take with me what I could carry on my back. A Jewish gypsy, they said. One more step into the unknown. Pack up, give away what I couldn't manage, but keep the palette knife and miniature easel. There was stuff happening back home. The boys were grown and earning a living. Their sister turned twenty-one. People were reinventing themselves all over the place then coming back home. A thousand train rides later, my mother nearly eighty. I won't be around much longer, she cried.

His was a helping hand in a world that says, but what are you doing there? What are you doing?

Undulations

So we're sitting in Melbourne in a vegan restaurant reminiscing about our schooldays spent mucking-up in the back row and Jane (her hair still red, short and frizzy, like childhood) remembers daring me to ask our fourth-grade geography teacher how to spell 'undulations'. What?

'Because I wanted to write her a message,' Jane says. 'An unsigned message saying, "The way you run your hands over your boobs to demonstrate undulations is disgusting," but didn't know how to spell it. So I told you that if you were my friend, you'd ask her. You know how she always said to speak up if we couldn't spell something? For some reason, she wrote the word down on a piece of paper, rather than on the blackboard. Maybe she thought you couldn't see properly from our eyrie. So you got back to your desk and passed it to me under the chair. I wrote in my best handwriting, "Your demonstrations of undulations are gross," blotted it carefully, and placed it furtively on her table after the recess bell had cleared the room. When we filed in after lunch, I saw her open it up.' Jane taps me on the arm enthusiastically.

'What happened then?' I say. 'Was she angry? Did she think it was me? Did I get punished?' How forgetful was I?

Jane had mastered the art of getting the ink from the inkwell to the pen nib to the paper, no ugly blotches, her cursive as good as a professional engraver's. Even after all this time, she still prefers a fountain pen and has a proclivity for setting wrongs right.

'She threw the chalk in the bin, reached for her cardigan and draped it over her shoulders,' Jane says, grinning. 'Yes, that's what happened. And she didn't demonstrate undulating landscapes on herself or on any of us ever again."

On Valentine's Day

You had to get out of them occasionally, those Australian country towns with the funny names: Wagga Wagga, Wee Waa, Woy Woy. Once, after a devastating week wiped out more than $4 trillion from the global stock exchanges, one of the local papers boasted a banner headline: WAGGA WAGGA WOMAN WEDS WOY WOY TOY BOY. You had to make an effort from time to time to get out, even if it meant flying all the way across the Nullarbor Plain to go to a Valentine's Day party.

In the centre of Wee Waa, across the road from a church and the grave yard was a small primary school and a scatter of classrooms used for adult education. For the last four years, Joanne Stephenson had been a teacher at the school. She loved those kids. At forty-two, with no relationship in sight, the probability of having a child of her own had become increasingly remote.

She also taught 'Vision Boarding As a Tool For Memoir Writing' in the evenings. She presented the course to men and to women, although attending the sessions and handing in the final assignment wouldn't help her students get a job. Even though her student evaluations had been slipping the last year or so – Joanne Stephenson has let everyone know in no uncertain terms how fed up she is with students arriving late for class or not doing their homework – all in all, the college was pleased to have her.

Living in Wee Waa was difficult for her, they knew. Once at the beginning of the year, she had turned all the lights off in the building and for twenty minutes had her students chant 'om' at the start of class. The manager had called her into his office, but did not say any words of criticism. Well, not exactly. Joanne Stephenson thinks cutting pictures out of magazines and pasting them into a scrapbook is a creative act. Is this an activity we should be paying for? He asked her how things were going and patted her on the wrist. She said, 'It's a big ask expecting adult students to sit in those tiny children's chairs,' and he studied the way she tightened the scarf at her neck as she said it. He wouldn't describe her as attractive, although her eyes were honest and reflected a willingness to listen mindfully when conversing with others. There wasn't enough effort with the untidy hair, though, and her scarves, worn so often to take the emphasis away from her face, were over the top, decorating her neck like a collage of bright parrot feathers.

'I'm losing my marbles in this place,' said Joanne to her younger sister, Penny in Perth. Joanne phoned her every Sunday.

'You're always harping on,' said Penny, 'but then you take yourself off somewhere and then you're happy to be back home to your routines and you're content for a while and say you have the perfect life, and then after a while you say you're pulling your hair out with boredom, and you start up with the whining again.'

Penny was a part-time caterer for the film industry. She'd turn up on location with her big food truck, set up trestle tables and canvas chairs in the middle of nowhere. She thought her life was 'pretty cool'. She was living with her husband of many years, who had recently taken a redundancy package. Penny and Henry had a twelve-year-old daughter, and recently moved to Perth from Sydney into a luxury high-rise apartment with large balconies overlooking the Swan River.

'We like to have friends over for barbecues on the balcony,' Penny was always gloating, as if to let Joanne know that, unlike her, she had a life outside of work.

It wasn't Penny's social life that made Joanne envious, however; it was the fact her sister had a child. Although the child's determined nature brought Penny to tears of frustration. This she didn't envy.

'Living away from the city has been good for my allergies,' said Joanne on the phone. She used to say it was to get away from petrol fumes, but now she said it was to avoid the dust mites. What have you run away from? a student once asked her. Bed bugs, she said and grinned. He looked dubious.

Her adult students were mostly salt-of-the-earth country people, spaced-out with endorphins from large quantities of good clean air. In class, they'd share stories of their childhood struggles, of adolescence, the death of loved ones. They seemed vulnerable at these times, often carrying a deep grief. She was good at encouraging them to open up on the page, but the outpouring of emotion that sometimes followed was difficult to contain. She wished she had the counselling skills to support them.

'I'm flying over to visit you next weekend,' announced Joanne.

'I was hoping you would,' said Penny. 'Henry and I are having a party for Valentine's Day. It falls on a Saturday this year. It should be fabulous. A dress-up party.'

'I'll dust off my devil horns and tail and shiny red tights.'

'Not that outfit again.'

'I've worn those horns so many times I'll probably end up giving birth with them on.'

'Ha ha,' laughed Penny. 'I really want you to come, but we've got a full house,' she apologised. 'All the beds are taken.'

'That's a shame.' Secretly, Joanne was relieved. She liked her own space, no matter how small. 'Don't worry, I'll book a hotel somewhere. And anyway, I don't like sleeping in other people's houses.'

'I'm not just anybody. I'm your sister. Next time you'll stay with us. Okay?'

'Okay.'

'You sure you haven't got anything else to wear? And for goodness sake, you're not expecting, are you?'

'No.'

'Unless there's someone in your life you haven't told us about?'

'I tell you everything. Why not be a single mum, though? It doesn't look like the whole marriage and baby thing's going to happen for me, so why not?'

'Don't do anything stupid.'

'You're only saying that because Virginia has always been a handful.'

'You're forty-two, woman. You've left your run too late. By the time you meet someone and decide to have a child, you'll be too old.

Should she say that one of her gay friends had said he'd help out if she decided to take the IVF option?

'You'd never be able to handle a baby on your own,' Penny had exploded once when Joanne had mentioned the possibility of going it alone. 'Without a guy, how would you manage?'

The thing was, Joanne hadn't given up on the whole baby thing. But she knew better than to say that to her sister.

That morning she'd woken up feeling decidedly unwell. It must have been the previous evening's pig-out on Indian food. She'd wondered, though, if that's what morning sickness would feel like.

Joanne had been out with two men since she'd come to Wee Waa. One of them was a tennis coach. 'Tennis is excellent for upper body strength,' her gynaecologist had told her. 'Fresh air and sunshine. It will do you good.' The tennis coach had stopped giving lessons when he fell and broke his wrist. He'd asked her out for a drink. At first she thought he was wonderful – someone who shared a common interest. But soon the tennis coach had become elusive and unreliable. One autumn day in his old Merc, when she'd asked him if there was a problem, he'd said, 'Have you tried wearing make-up?' She'd stopped using cosmetics since the allergies. She brushed a leaf out of her hair.

'And don't leave that on the floor,' he said, driving. 'You know the rule about eating in the car.'

She rolled her eyes and sighed deeply. 'I wasn't eating a leaf, for goodness sake.'

He slowed down at an amber light and frowned. 'Same thing. No crumbs, no bits of anything to be cleaned up.'

'Oh really! You're so anal!'

The second guy was more of a realist, more practical. His name was Joe Maddigan and he cleaned the windows in her three-storey walk-up. His ladder couldn't reach her top-floor unit, so he had to get her phone number to arrange a suitable time to come and clean the outsides of the windows by hanging out the window ledge. One evening when he'd forgotten to collect his cleaning rags, she'd had to let him in again. He'd said something about missing the last train, so she'd let him stay over, after he'd promised to sleep on the couch. In the end, they'd both slept on the sofa. She'd dated him for a few months, but the thing was, what did they have in common? He was on the outside looking in and she was on the inside looking out.

'There's something I have to ask you,' said Penny. 'I know there's meant to be a man-drought but I meet plenty of men.'

'What are you saying?'

'Are you dating anyone? I'm asking for a reason, I'm not just like Dad was.'

Dad. Good old Dad. He couldn't understand why Joanne wasn't married. It brought back painful memories. The smell of urine in the old family house when he had become decrepit with dementia to the point that their mother had to place him in a home, then two years later, the death of Mother from cancer. We're orphans now, Penny had said.

'I'm dating myself. I take myself to the movies, or out for a walk.'

'The reason I'm asking is that I know someone I think you could be interested in,' said Penny. 'He's a laugh a minute. Fun. Heterosexual. Not currently married. That's about it.'

'I don't tend to do things just for fun. I want to come over, sit on your balcony and watch black swans on the river.'

'Well, whatever you like. You can do both. Play it by ear. Don't forget your devil's outfit,' said Penny.

'I take those red stockings with me everywhere.'

Joanne found a hotel overlooking the jetty, with its row of ferries bound for Rottnest Island. The few scattered shops, cafés and restaurants were set in between the road works that Perth council had promised would transform the area. A woman her own age manned the reception desk. This woman gave her the key to a cheap, old-fashioned room on the top floor. There were a multitude of grimy windows that could keep someone like Joe Maddigan very busy. She brought to mind his soft face and the way his chin gathered into a dimple when he smiled. She'd always been a sucker for young and cute. How many weeks had it been?

She went for a walk along the marina's boardwalk and then up the steep steps behind the hotel that led to Kings Park and the Botanic Gardens. Bold banksias, boronias and kangaroo paws as she made her way to the top, where she could see the city skyline and the Swan River. The western coast was just like she'd remembered it: native orchids, Federation houses, the light of the sun setting into the ocean. What would it be like to live there? She kept herself occupied with the mathematics of what another move would entail, and also with ideas of how to earn money in some different way, a contrast to all the things she'd done before. Working in a shop would be monotonous, but reception could be okay. How much an hour would a hotel receptionist get paid? She wouldn't mind being cut off, living in Australia's most remote city. After all, that's where her sister lived.

A coffee bar overlooked the boardwalk at the hotel, but only one man was there eating bacon and eggs. A waiter came in from the kitchen with a tea towel over his arm. He asked Joanne's room number and led her to the bench where the man was sitting. The man had a lean face, a greyish-blonde moustache and a downcast look. He glanced up as she approached and moved his newspaper to the side to make room for her. It was open at the sports pages. Like Joe Maddigan, who only looked at the back pages. The man gave her a friendly nod and made a comment about the sunny weather. She smiled back at him, hoping to avoid seeing any fried egg caught between his teeth. She tried to joke about the weather being perfect for all the romantics on Valentine's Day. They exchanged information on things to see and do in Perth. He suggested she catch a ferry to Rottnest Island to see the quokkas. He wouldn't mind going there again himself, if she wanted some company.

When he finished his breakfast, he stood up and handed her his newspaper. 'Just for you,' he said with a smile.

'At last!' Penny yelled through the intercom, before the click of the security gate of her sister's block of units.

Joanne took the lift to the nineteenth floor, where Penny was waiting at the wide open door. Joanne stepped in and hugged her sister close. Twelve-year-old Virginia was lying on the couch in front of the television behind them.

'This is how you do it,' Penny said over her shoulder to Virginia.

'She's still not hugging then?' Joanne whispered.

'No. See, Virginia,' Penny said louder, 'you put your arms around each other, maybe rock from side to side, then a little pat on the back.'

'Was she watching us?' asked Joanne. Penny had told her about Virginia's recent aversion to affection. Maybe leaving her friends and school behind had made her resentful.

'Out of the corner of her eye, I think.'

The apartment was open and light, with a view across the river of the city.

'It's great to see you,' said Joanne.

'Say hello to Aunty Joanne.'

'Hello, darling,' Joanne called out to the girl, who mumbled a greeting in return.

'Now, what would you like?' said Penny. 'Cup of tea?'

Penny made them tea and a snack – toasted cheese on Turkish – and carried a tray out to the balcony.

'So how's life with Henry now he's home all the time now?' asked Joanne.

'To tell you the truth, I'm used to my freedom. None of this coming home in the middle of the day to make lunch.'

Joanne nodded with understanding. 'If you're not working, you want to be out playing tennis. Right?'

'Exactly.'

'What is it people say? I married him for life, not for lunch. Something like that.'

'Yeah. But the thing is, I worry about Virginia. She's a real home body. She doesn't want to leave the apartment. It's just so hard to get her out the door.'

'Oh,' said Joanne. 'I know how she feels.' She leaned back on the woven-cane couch and stared pensively across the river. It seemed unnatural for a kid to be living up in the air like this, no backyard to kick a ball around in. Although there was the indoor heated lap pool.

Penny sighed. 'She comes home from school and just wants to veg out on the couch.'

Joanne sat up and adjusted the cushions behind her back. 'What's wrong with that?' she said, in a firm, maternal way. She rubbed her sister's arm, gently, as if to reassure her.

'Really? You think that's okay?' Penny smiled with relief.

'Kids have a lot of pressure on them these days. There's no harm in unwinding on the sofa but I find the longer I sit on the couch, the harder it is to get up.'

She thought now of herself, solitary in her apartment; of the pesky flies that multiplied like crazy in the holes between the bricks on her terrace, landing on her coffee table, thirsty; of the second toothbrush she kept in the container with the toothpaste in her bathroom, that someone had told her would make any tradespeople think she didn't live alone.

After lunch, Joanne joined her niece on the lounge, leaving Penny to do the final clean-up before the party.

'I don't need your help,' she'd said. 'You know how I like to do things my way.'

Virginia was playing a game of tennis on the Wii through the television monitor. She had a determined but fine-boned face, and long straight hair. She wore a pink and white all-in-one rabbit suit.

'You're still in your pyjamas?' said Joanne.

'When I got up, it was lying on the floor, so I put it on.'

'She doesn't like getting dressed,' Penny called out from the kitchen.

Sitting on the couch watching Virginia move on from tennis to golf, then tenpin bowling and finally, figure skating, Joanne glanced over at a packet of chocolate mint biscuits on the back of the lounge that Virginia had been munching between games. Joanne stood up and motioned toward the biscuits with raised eyebrows to indicate that she'd like to have one. Virginia, silent, scowled at her aunt then shook her head, 'No.'

All the same, Joanne felt comforted being there with her sister and niece. When Virginia finished playing on the Wii, she picked up the biscuits, took them with her to her bedroom and closed the door.

Joanne reached inside her bag for her crochet hook and yarn. So this was what she'd become: a woman sitting in front of the television, crocheting.

At the Valentine's party, about forty people showed up. There were people in organza tutus, genie princesses, belly dancers and schoolboys. There was a cupid carrying a bow and a group of burlesque ballerinas. Penny and Henry were in their heart lock-and-key-couples costume.

Henry had a huge blow-up gold key hanging around his neck. 'Joanne! Long time, no see. Sorry I wasn't here to greet you this afternoon.' After that, he went off to take photos of the belly dancers and the ballerinas.

'Is there anything you'd like me to do?' Joanne asked her sister. 'You've put on a fabulous party. You must be exhausted.' She patted

Penny's shoulder, softly, as if she wished they could go off somewhere, just the two of them.

'Actually, you know what?'

'What?' Joanne adjusted her flashing devil horns in the tangles of her curly hair.

'You know what you can do?' said Penny, arranging slices of eggplant on the grill. 'Meet Robert. He's the bloke I wanted you to meet. When he gets here, make him feel included. He's a good guy but he's in recovery from a bitter divorce.'

'Okay,' Joanne sighed. 'I'll do what I can.'

When Robert arrived, he was wearing a light-up red bow tie and sweetheart-shaped red glasses – cute.

'Joanne, this is Robert,' said Penny.

'Hi,' said Robert, reaching out to shake her hand. He stared at the blinking horns on her head. 'Very eye-catching!'

Joanne nodded. 'Love the glasses,' she said. She looked past him, out the sliding glass doors to the city high-rises reflected in the water; people were making the usual comments: how it looked like a fairyland out there, magic castles in the air. 'There's Peroni out on the terrace, Robert – would you like one?' Joanne asked.

'Sure. I'll come outside with you.'

They edged past the other guests, passing a schoolboy and the cupid. The sliding door gave way in a rush, and Joanne and Robert stepped out onto the balcony, a little red devil and a spectacled romantic. The air reverberated with cool unpredictability. Joanne found the plastic esky, burrowed into it and salvaged two beers.

'Thanks,' said Robert. His bow tie sparkled as he twisted open the bottle. 'Penny tells me you're a tutor. Where do you teach?'

'In Wee Waa, New South Wales.'

He looked surprised. 'Penny didn't tell me that bit. I'm a production manager in the film business,' he said. His cheeks were starting to redden, his glasses skew whiff on his head.

'Do you like it?'

'Yes.' A grin, a lopsided one. 'Not much money in freelance, though.' He shifted his weight to his other leg. 'Are you dating anyone?'

'Now? This minute?'

'Obviously not at this very moment.' He gave her a puzzled look.

Below them, a ferry slid in to the old wooden dock with a gentle clunk.

'No. But since living in Wee Waa I've dated a tennis coach and a window cleaner.' she said. 'Jason and Joe. Things didn't seem to work out with either of them. What about you?'

He told her about the split-up with his wife and how they'd been trying to have a baby for years. Now his ex-wife was waiting for him to give approval to the laboratory to destroy their unused fertilised eggs. The breeze moistened his eyes.

Joanne looked at him sympathetically. 'That's terrible. What an awful decision to have to make.'

All the time he was talking, she was trying to think what his way of speaking reminded her of. It wasn't one particular person, although she might have had one or two students in Wee Waa who spoke with the same rhythms, the inflection at the end of a sentence, the dropping of the 'g' sound at the end of a word.

She wished she could think of something else to say. All she could think about was a childless woman like herself somewhere, desperate to implant those eggs.

'Want some nibbles?' Penny edged through the sliding door. She thrust forward a plate of grilled eggplant in one hand and napkins in the other.

'Yum,' said Robert, enthusiastically. He seemed fond of Penny, and put his arm around her shoulder.

'Where's Virginia?' asked Joanne.

Penny made a face. 'In her room. Where else would she be?'

'It must be the adolescent mood swings,' said Joanne.

She remembered when the whole family had been living in Sydney. She would pop in to Penny and Henry's house every day after work to see her niece. And every weekend too. She adored the little girl. 'Go home and start your own family,' Henry would say in irritation.

'You know, I'll be back in a minute,' Joanne said now.

'Okay,' said Robert, looking perturbed. 'If you must.'

Joanne hurried inside, across the lounge room, down the hallway toward Virginia's bedroom. She knocked gently on the door, then walked in. Virginia was sitting in bed, headphones plugged into her ears. Joanne flicked on the light. Virginia looked up and indicated with a lift of her eyelids that it was okay for Joanne to enter.

Joanne leant closer to the girl, put her arms around her, placed her lips on her hair. 'Don't worry; I won't kiss you. I'm going now. I just came in to say goodnight.'

Virginia remained silent but gave a little smile.

'See you soon,' Joanne said, before leaving the room.

She closed the door behind her. Maybe she wouldn't be up to the task of handling a moody child. It might be beyond her capabilities.

Joanne read for half an hour before climbing into bed. Then she went down the hall to the bathroom. It was well past midnight. The rest of the hotel was in darkness. She had left her door slightly ajar and, returning to her room, she did not turn on the corridor light. The door diagonally opposite was also ajar and, as she was passing she heard someone whisper. She recognised the moustache and long face with tucked-in chin of the man who had given her his newspaper. He was lying on the bed watching her from his dark room and he gestured at her to come in. She ignored him and headed for her own room, shut the door and locked it.

She lay there awake for most of the night. She knew that there was a time when she might have considered walking into that room, and earlier that evening she could have given a signal to Robert. Not so long ago she might have done – or she might not have done, depending on how she felt at the time. Now it felt like an impossibility.

After all, she was in a new and unusual condition. Her body was holding a secret, a secret she wasn't going to tell.

Alfresco

She remembers the exact moment she agreed to go to the midwinter yoga retreat. Her friend Vivian had been there before and said she would come back a new person. Transformed.

According to the brochure, 'The gentle trilling from an orchestra of insects interspersed with the croaking of frogs and the occasional haunting cries of owls will be a soothing and entirely natural symphony to fall asleep to.'

They'd sleep in secluded forest huts nestled in the tropical rainforest canopy. She was ready to pack her bags when she read that an optional extra was to book an alfresco en suite. Alfresco en suite? Better than no en suite, in the middle of the night, in the middle of a jungle.

*

The sun is shining when they take a logo-painted van from Cairns airport to the retreat. On the way, everything looks picture-postcard perfect. Clear blue skies, white-sand beaches, rows of palm trees. Tropical north Queensland. Exactly what she had in mind. A four-wheel drive vehicle transports them from the car park across the delicate forest floor to a natural clearing where they are ushered in to Reception. A few loosely robed yogis are in a glass-walled, timber-floored restaurant. Beyond it, a beach beneath the rainforest canopy and an unsettled sea. 'Watch the moon appear out of the ocean from the elevated balcony.'

Accessed by a boardwalk, her hut, with its lack of solid walls, at first glance seems filled with the cool, green light of the rainforest, a cubbyhouse in the trees. The timber structure is screened on all four sides with curtains. Her cold-water bathroom is on a deck that extends from the hut with shower, basin and toilet sheltered by the foliage of the forest. Cold water? Maybe the middle of winter wasn't such a good idea. The bed, however, with its bright white linen cover and matching plumped-up cushions, looks huge and inviting. She takes off her shoes and enjoys the bounce as she flattens out on her back. Next door Vivian is changing into lycra tights for a quick jog before the Welcome Meetup. She leans back on the down pillows, sleepy already.

At five o'clock, all new yogis are invited into a light-filled studio with mirrored wall. American Matthew, their dedicated Buddhist and meditation guru, says they can choose their level of postures to strengthen and limber their bodies: strong and dynamic or gentle and restorative. She knows Vivian, with her over-achiever personality, will choose the hardest option. She'll go for the easiest.

'Be daring and push your limits,' says Matthew, with his generous nose, astonishing white teeth and bitten-to-the-quick nails.

Not what she had in mind.

Before they head back to their rooms, Matthew warns them that if they hear a loud noise during the night that sounds like a bomb dropping, don't worry. It could be a male owl inflating the skin around his neck to create a booming sound. Just like a bomb falling.

Amazingly, she sleeps well, considering the cacophony of strange noises in the night and the challenge of using the outside loo. No sound of bombs dropping so far. Surprisingly, the cold water in the shower is warm.

Their first practice of the day is to align their chakras before meditation: the push-up of the brain. A Tibetan bell announces the commencement of class.

'Leave your egos at the door,' says Matthew. 'No comparing yourself to others.'

So here she sits, on a mat imagining a piece of string running from the base of her spine up her back and out the top of her head, pulling her upright. She's tuning into what is going on outside the room – people walking past, birds chirping, the sound of the wind through the forest.

And all around, the colourful birds hop among the tree branches calling out to each other: she could swear they are trying to warn them about something.

That evening, after a salad of slow-cooked lamb smothered in caramelised onion, they treat themselves and order a bottle of Beaujolais. It's the first drink they've had since leaving Sydney, apart from water with mint leaves thrown in and a green smoothie. Caffeine and alcohol are freely available. She drinks carefully, aware of the disintegration of the bottle's cork and possible cork crumble in the wine. The glass is small and she takes pleasure in the fine clear red of the Beaujolais, telling herself not to let its vinegar aftertaste plunge her into negativity.

The biting midges drive her crazy. At five a.m. she wakes from a heavy, fear-filled sleep, feeling frantic after having lost sight of her children in the dream as they cycled away and out of view. She hadn't known how to use her new mobile, so was unable to make contact with them. What would her grown-up children, the products of an early marriage, say about her being here? 'You mean you're on one of those crazy retreat things again?' Should she have spent all this money on herself? What was she thinking? Transformation? A bit late in the day for that.

Each day is basically the same but her thinking is spiralling inwards and downwards. She longs to retreat to her room and just read a book.

Some people do extra stretching on the beach, others are attached to their devices on the free wifi near the restaurant. This whole 'alfresco thing' with no walls to the treehouses, the billowing curtains letting in the bugs, is a challenge. Roll-on repellent, mosquito coils and anti-itch cream don't help.

Matthew has been doing his best to guide them through the

Buddha's teachings. He doesn't need to tell them the first two of the Buddha's Four Noble Truths.

Dukkha: Suffering Exists

Samudaya: There is a cause for suffering.

The warm inner glow that he talks about has not enveloped her. In fact, his new-age-speak is grating on her nerves.

If another person says, 'How's your day been going so far?' she'll scream.

On the way to her treehouse, she notices Matthew as, partially covered by a towel, he steps out of the alfresco shower to the edge of his balcony. He turns to face the sun and dries his toned naked body. He describes himself as a 'nomad' and talks about his life spent travelling in search of deeper spiritual meaning and 'the stillness'. His seductive movements with the towel remind her of one of those male strippers in Magic Mike. She makes a mental note to keep her eyes open in the yoga class when he says to shut them and then walks around making 'adjustments' to their poses.

She tries to share her concerns about Matthew with Vivian, who snaps, 'Don't disillusion me. He's wonderful, and very handsome too.' No point in arguing with her.

Was it philosopher Jean-Paul Sartre who said, 'Hell is other people'?

Vivian is the more sociable of the two, but gets irritated with Ms Never-Shuts-Up Tattooist. A skinny, gum-chewing, permanently plugged-into-headphones 'woman-who-lives-in-a-van', in sports bra and tights, a colourful crocheted beanie on top of her copper-tipped blonde hair. While they peruse pictures of her ink designs on her iPad, she tells them she got her first tattoo at seventeen. She was living with her grandparents and wanted to shock them. The tattoo is spread across her chest with a lock at her heart.

'What about you two?' she says. 'Would you get a tatt?'

'When you get older, your skin wrinkles,' says Vivian. 'And so does the tatt. So, no.'

Then the colourful tattooist with the crochet beanie drifts on to another table and leaves them to discuss the merits of living in a van, becoming a nomad, or turning into a hermit.

After breakfast, Vivian suggests they go down to the swimming hole, a tranquil pool hidden deep in the forest. They grab costumes and towels and head out.

The walking trail meanders through the rainforest across a trickling creek and through a shielded gully. The banks of the creek flourish with ferns and sweet-smelling white native jasmine and a choir of croaking green-eyed tree frogs.

'When the frogs croak like that, it means rain is on the way,' says Vivian.

'A walk is so relaxing.'

'Red wine is relaxing,' says Vivian. 'You should drink more of it,' she adds, in an unpleasant tone of voice.

'Have you seen yourself when you're drunk? Not a pretty picture.'

There's no point in bickering.

Another shocking night. At four a.m., too early to get up, a long, harsh scream erupts from the ceiling. Heart thumping, she throws her pillow towards the sound, then sits up in the dark and swears. She can't go on another day. By concentrating hard on the rafters above her, she can make out a white-lipped green tree frog clinging to the wood. Was it you who was making those horrible noises? she asks it.

At six a.m., she meets up with Vivian for an early breakfast. 'I'm an absolute wreck. I hardly slept. In the night, I thought, I could just throw myself off the balcony.'

Vivian looks at her wearily.

'Want to see if we can book an earlier flight home?'

Hesitation. Vivian's jaw clenches. 'No. There's no going back early. And don't forget, we're in this together.'

'Together? You go off each day and do your own thing and I do mine. You like being in the sun, I like the shade. You're on the beach, I'm in the hut.'

They march in to breakfast.

'I shouldn't have agreed to come to this place in midwinter,' she mutters to Gerry (pronounced Jeree), a cheeky American know-it-all in his seventies with grey curly hair and thick silver bangles inlaid with jade. He likes to boast that he lives part of the year in Florida and the other half in Kent in the UK. 'Bridge, golf and tennis.' he tells people.

'Ah,' his eyes twinkle wisely, 'if you'd lived in as many countries as I have, you'd know to expect this. You haven't learnt to go with the flow. You still get caught up in irritability and impatience. A common first-world problem.'

What's he talking about? She stomps away to the café bar and orders a large latte. Anthony, the cook from New York, tells her the long scream in the night was probably one of the frogs. Yes, she knows that.

In the afternoon, sitting on the beach with Vivian, they watch as the colourful tattooist, her blonde locks splaying on to her shoulders, appears shimmering from a swim in the sea and walks leisurely back to her towel. The young woman lies on her front, unhooks her bikini top, then turns over and sits up so they can see the expanse of her back gleaming in the sun. There, covering the whole area is a giant tiger head tattoo.

'See,' says Vivian. 'A leopard can change its spots. It can turn itself into a tiger, with stripes.'

The artwork is so beautifully executed, so lifelike, so spellbinding, the tiger's head so intricately and boldly defined, so regal and powerful, that they find themselves forgetting their differences and contemplating the transformative power of getting inked.

Departure day is fast approaching. Why not skip the classes and go for a long walk? Walking, she finds, sets just the right rhythm for the sort of thinking she likes to do. She makes her way up to the front gate, past the majestic rosewood trees and an array of multicoloured birds swooping through the forest. It has rained in the night, and snails, grey and lilac, adorn the sandstone path. She heads out to the swimming hole, but today she takes a different path, not the one towards the little bridge, but one that leads more steeply down the hill, a quicker descent to the bottom of the gully and the deep pool.

The rain has muddied the water but all around her are shallow layers of multicoloured pebbles. Never has she seen such a variety of stones, shape-shifting beneath her feet as she walks along the water's edge. She marvels at their diversity, each pebble like the next one – only different. How many years of tumbling has it taken to become so perfectly smooth and round? She glances around and, seeing no one, undresses and carefully steps across the shiny pebbles. She walks out into the water. It is so much warmer than she expected. When she is waist deep, she sucks in a breath, plunges in and swims toward the other bank. Being here, she tells herself, is exactly what she should be doing in life, right now. She looks up to the sky and gives thanks.

As she strides back through the grey-green wilderness, she's aware of an easing within herself. She can see it. An acceptance of the way things are. And with this acceptance comes the comforting realisation that she is at peace with herself, but the old self, not a new transformed one.

Jean-Pierre

This was in a far distant land. There were pilates classes but no surfing beaches or vegan restaurants. People said to hell with low-fat diets and tiny portions.

Charles, who had wanted her to hire his friend Jean-Pierre as tour guide, had encouraged her in yoga class. 'Look, Zina, you're a facilitator. You've been running those groups for what – thirty years?'

'Only twenty, for goodness sake.' She had turned forty-nine and frowned at him upside down between the legs of a downward facing dog. She had a face marked by the sun, a face left to wrinkle and form crevasses by years of smoking, a face made shiny by the application of six drops of jojoba oil, although the shop girl had recommended she use only three. 'I love that word facilitator. It says so much.'

'Twenty. All right. This guy's not at all your type. He's a numbers man. He shows tourists around in between engineering contracts. He can show you how to buy a bus or a train ticket, how to withdraw money out of the wall, get your bearings. You can hire him for half a day. Or, in your case, half a day and half the night.'

'Very funny,' she said, stifling a laugh.

Now they were on all fours arching their backs like cats, then flattening their spines to warm up the discs. Indian chanting music took your mind off the fact that the person behind you was confronted with your broad derriere.

'So what's the story with Jean-Pierre?'

'Someone I met at a conference in Monaco,' said Charles on an out-breath. 'Large-yacht communications. He's charismatic, let me tell you.' Charles dyed his hair and beard a rich brown, and in yoga class it stood on end to reveal a circle of grey at the crown. He had paid many visits to this far away country since he started learning the language.

She'd never had the courage to have a go herself. She knew how to say, 'Good morning, madame,' every time she walked into a shop, how to ask for the bill, how to say please and thank you. What else did you need? Charles had moved on to German classes and was planning a trip to Berlin with his wife. They were even taking their two kids. Toledo and Paris they called them.

'Look, you're going to the land of endless rail strikes,' Charles said. 'You'll need Jean-Pierre, or you'll be stranded on train platforms, not knowing what to do or where to go.'

'Come on, now. You're such an exaggerator. They're not always on strike.'

They lay on their backs, legs wide open in the air in a happy baby pose.

'All right, I suppose so,' she said. 'You can give me his email address.'

'I love croissants and baguettes and all of that,' said Charles, sighing over his shoulder.

The yoga instructor was walking around the room, checking out their poses and had reached the back row. 'Focus inwards, be in the moment,' he reprimanded Zina and Charles. 'Let the soles of your feet reach for the ceiling,' he said before returning to the stage to demonstrate the cosmic egg. He eased his face between his thighs. 'Now bury your eye sockets into your kneecaps.'

'I'm not trying to fix you up with JP,' Charles whispered. 'I really hate that kind of thing.' He twinkled across at her.

'Lift your hips high off the mat and boom your heart toward the back wall.'

Jean-Pierre was still charismatic and, on close examination, was still handsome. About sixty, with a splendid head of hair. His face was persuasive, his forehead, his large nose. They ate croissants at Cosmo, the busiest café in the village. She drank green tea infused with fresh mint, the leaves determined to block the spout of the teapot.

Jean-Pierre sipped on an espresso. He nodded at her tea. 'English,' he said with a note of barely disguised distain. 'The English drink tea.'

She bristled. A racist. A narrow-minded, insular, arrogant racist.

She looked at his intense face as he stroked the black and white head of his dog, who peeped out above the zip of his jacket, and felt sorry for his preconceptions and a little sorry for herself when she reflected on it, because, really, he seemed to know very little about Australia. Do you have black Africans living off social security? Poor Jean-Pierre didn't know an African from an Aborigine.

'No, green tea is not English,' she said haughtily, giving him the evil eye, to show him, to show him this: 'Green tea originated in China.'

'Madame?' said the waiter, reaching for her empty plate.

'Merci,' she nodded.

'Did you fly Business?' Jean-Pierre said abruptly. 'Such a long flight from Australia.'

'Economy. I'm a poor struggling facilitator.'

'You have to get out there and promote your courses. Then you can fly Business.'

'We don't all do things just for the money.'

Jean-Pierre looked down the narrow cobbled pedestrian-only street. 'There are two things you must watch out for here,' he said. 'The motorbikes…and the dog poo.'

'Thanks,' she said, then, trying to be friendly, 'In New York they say you can tell the tourists from the locals because the tourists are the ones looking up at the skyscrapers and the locals are the ones looking down for the dog poo.'

He twisted the gold band that girded the blowsy fat of his finger. 'I was married to a New York lawyer once. Very clever. She read four books a week. I read only one a month. Are you married?'

'Not currently.'

'My son speaks four languages,' said Jean-Pierre. 'My mother likes to say that anyone can get a Masters, but if you've got four languages, rather than three, you'll be a success in life. I've only got three. What about you? Any children?'

Eli had stayed at her place for the week just before she left home. He'd sat in the lounge room, eyes fixed to his iPad. She would sometimes watch on as he played a combat game. He'd build a village, train his troops and take them into battle. She would watch his face deep in concentration, so focused he seemed unable to hear when she asked him to set the table, or unstack the dishwasher. She didn't like the every-second-week deal with his father, so disruptive to getting a routine in place. Eli would come with her to the gym sometimes, or they'd go for a jog around the oval. It's not as if his father did any of those things. She did her best: drove Eli to cricket and footy, helped with his homework, listened whenever he was willing to talk, always made sure there was meat in the house when it was her week 'on'. Eli said to her, 'When you and Dad were together, we always ate with the TV turned off. Now you're divorced, you and me can eat dinner in front of the telly if we feel like it. Much better.'

'Yes,' she said to Jean-Pierre. 'I have a son.'

'It's different in this country. We're Catholics. We don't usually divorce. Not when there are children. Are you a Catholic?'

'No.'

'Religious?'

'Spiritual, but not religious. We could do with less religion in the world, in my opinion. Why?'

'I was going to suggest I show you the island of Saint Honorat off Antibes, but tourists only go there in order to see the sacred abbey. The thing is, I grew up in Antibes. I know it like the back of my hand. I could hire a car and we can drive to different parts that the tourists don't see. We can spend a few hours in Antibes, then, after that, if you want, we can have lunch. What do you think?'

'What would it cost?'

'Well, there's the cost of the car, then my time. So…all up, a hundred and eighty euros.

'I'll give it some thought.'

Jean-Pierre lowered his dog to the ground, reached for his wallet, pulled out a ten-euro note and placed it on the edge of the table for the waiter.

She unzipped her handbag to pay her share but he patted her on the arm and said proudly, 'No. No. Put your money away. I'm a Frenchman.'

The second time they met up, they went for a walk into Nice via the foreshore. It was a difficult walk. Eighty sets of steps interspersed with slippery limestone rocks. When she asked why the gate was locked at the end of the walk, necessitating a dangerous climb over a high fence on the edge of a cliff, Jean-Pierre said the authorities probably kept the gate locked because they didn't want tourists getting washed off the rocks at high tide. It wasn't a good look.

Now he wanted to have lunch at the port.

'Where do you like to eat?' she asked.

She was still thinking about the climb over the gate, when she'd been so afraid that she wouldn't be able to get her leg high enough and would crash to an early death on the rocks below. She'd needed to sit on the stone wall to compose herself afterwards. It was Jean-Pierre who had acknowledged her courage, had said she'd done well, that she'd even looked graceful when she'd executed the tricky manoeuvre and swung herself out into the void before throwing herself over the top. Before they'd left on the walk, he'd told her he hadn't followed the coastline into Nice for a long time, and was really looking forward to walking it again. He wouldn't be charging her his usual hourly rate, as it was something he'd been wanting to do for ages. 'My wife kept me on a tight leash.'

'There are plenty of places to eat at the port,' he said.

They walked down the hill and he leaned in and gave her shoulder a quick squeeze. 'You did well,' he repeated.

She blushed with embarrassment at the intimacy of his gesture. She'd only just met him, after all. And anyway, she was no good at relationships. There were people she knew who were good at them and people who weren't. She was no good.

'What sort of restaurant do you like to lunch at back home?' he said.

'We mostly don't have a big meal in the middle of the day.'

'No? What do you do?'

'Well, um, we usually jog around the park, then stand in line to order large skimmed lattes.'

'Ah,' he said, and put his hand over hers where it rested on the table. She felt her hand go still like a frightened animal. Jean-Pierre's hand was rough and warm as it lay over hers. Maybe she shouldn't have drunk two beers in the middle of the day.

On Saturday afternoon, Jean-Pierre took her and a group of American tourists by ferry to an old island prison. 'You'll find this place worth a visit,' he said, as they waited on the wharf. 'An infamous jail for deportees, prisoners convicted of political crimes, such as espionage or conspiracy.'

'Interesting,' she said, stepping across the gangplank. She sat down beside Jean-Pierre at the front of the boat.

The four American couples filed down to the back row of seats. 'We can throw Smarties at you from here,' one of them joked.

Jean-Pierre tapped on her sunshade. 'You won't need this. It's dark in the cells.' He pulled a map out of his pocket and opened it out, pointing to the layout of the buildings. 'The locations of the public toilets,' he said. 'That's what every tour guide needs to know.' He folded up his map and put it in his breast pocket. 'I want to give you a quick kiss now, before we get into one of those dark cells,' he said. 'I won't be able to see you in there.'

He turned towards her, and suddenly his face, up very close, appeared at the end of her nose, floating, as she leant against the back of the seat. He shut his eyes and kissed her, soft and probing, and she kept her sunshade on for privacy, lips, mouth, teeth and tongue, his hand moving very slowly up her arm, up to her shoulder and to her bare neck, and hovered there for only a moment, cradling her face, before he moved away, straightened his trousers, and quietly pulled out his map again.

She adjusted herself and stared out the window to the water. Jean-Pierre gave the signal that they were nearing their destination and to prepare for disembarkation.

'We don't do things like that in Sydney,' murmured Zina. She refreshed her lipstick.

'No?' Jean-Pierre grinned and levelled out her visor.

'No, it's um, all those coffees. You just keep running. Forever and ever. You spend your whole life,' her hands juggled an imaginary t'ai chi ball, 'on the run.'

Well-kept concrete walkways led up, over and around the island's hill.

Jean-Pierre steered them through a rustic entrance to the old prison complex. 'And now,' he said, 'we come to that part of our tour most likely to give you claustrophobia. The Reclusion Disciplinaire area.'

They stepped up and through a narrow hallway toward the low, dark solitary confinement cells.

'This is where prisoners were kept in silence and darkness,' Jean-Pierre was saying. He led the way into the dark of the single-person cells. 'You won't be able to see a thing in there.'

She squinted ahead at the front of the group, which had now gathered by the doorway. It looked scary. She took off her sunglasses and shade, but could see nothing as she stepped in. The blackness lay heavily all around, not like a moonless sky, but like a creepy cupboard with stone walls and low roof, a stone tomb. There was something inhuman in the cruelty of the space, a place where the light never shone, hidden, despair-inducing.

'I'm right behind you,' Jean-Pierre said, moving close, 'in case you're frightened.' He gave her hand a squeeze, then placed his arm around her waist.

She could smell his aftershave – or was it cologne? – feel the warmth of his breath on her neck, and leaned, unseeing and anxious, into his body. She reached for his arm and clutched at his hand where it rested on her waist.

*

When they went to bed together, she almost broke into joyous laughter. He'd drawn her in without even trying. His face, his voice, his eyes. It was a whole-package thing. He made her feel so special. He was more appreciative than anyone she had ever known. He hugged and kissed and even offered to go downstairs and get her cigarettes out of her handbag.

He got out of bed and went over to the piano. He fumbled with some sheet music in the semi-dark, holding each up to the light until he found what he wanted. 'I play this sometimes,' he said, in a quiet voice. 'It starts with a single note, a B natural, growing in dynamic from a soft pianissimo to a very loud fortissimo.'

She listened as he played the one note, building up to full strength. Who was this guy?

When he'd finished, he turned to her and said, 'Especially for you. I use my music to express my feelings.'

They made love again. Once more he got out of bed and sat beneath the black and white photograph of himself with his mother and his brother. He began to play. After a while, he stopped playing and went into the bathroom to wash his hands. When he returned, he wore the hand towel looped over his erect penis. She rolled over to have a look and kissed him, his face glowing with pride.

Morning. The bakeries were laying out their breads and pastries filling the air with the mouth-watering aroma of freshly baked baguettes. In the antique shop windows, as the sun struck them, the cleaners hosed the cobbled alleys.

Jean-Pierre rose early and walked to the boulangerie. He laid the breakfast out on a tray and brought it in to her in bed. Outside the window, the sky was a clear faded blue, and patches of sun, geometric designs of light, streaked the doona. He put the tray on the bed, and she sat up and stroked his face, his skin still chilled from the morning air.

She pointed at the pain au chocolat. 'So I need to forget about the diet?'

'*Oui.*' His mouth was already filled with pastry, chocolate oozing between his lips. 'It's good for you. Don't you know that the flour in this country is so good, and so different, that even gluten-intolerant people can eat the bread and quiches?'

Her workshops, as she wrote to Eli back home, were going well. She'd managed to book a space in an old sixteenth-century citadel overlooking the Mediterranean. And she'd made a new friend. Something had happened to her in an old isolation cell, she didn't know what exactly. But she had to get back home. I hope you and Dad are getting on okay and he hasn't had any more nasty blow-ups. It's a mild winter here. Some people are even swimming and sunbaking on the beach. Love, Mum.

They went on the bus to visit his mother, the music of Bach on a score above his head. In Bach there was not only symmetry and logic but more, a system, a reiteration which everything hinged on. His hair was uncombed. His face had the modesty, the unpretentious lips of someone secretly able to calculate the frequencies of the string vibrations.

His mother met him at the door and took his dark face in her hands. She stepped back to see better. 'Your hair,' she said.

He combed it down with his fingers.

His brother came from the kitchen to embrace him. 'Where have you been?' he cried.

At night, Jean-Pierre began to sleep with one hand resting on her solar plexus, the other curled around her shoulder, as if to shield her from bad dreams.

When she slept against him like that, her life on the other side of the world crumpled into her backpack that hung on a hook behind the door. Could she live the rest of her life in a far-away-country? Maybe she could. Except for that funny feeling in the pit of her. Like a rock in the guts.

On Sunday morning, Jean-Pierre took her for a walk up to Mont Baron. 'You'll love the view from the old fort,' he said. 'You can see Italy to the left and Nice to the right.'

'Sounds wonderful!' she said, closing the door behind them.

They climbed the steep steps that led up the hill. The sky was gold with light.

'Why don't you come with me to Australia?' she said.

'I don't think so.'

She listened to the sound of water over rocks.

'No?' she said.

He was silent. After a moment, he said, 'I can't.'

She began to imagine she could hear the sound of a kookaburra laughing.

'No,' she said. 'I think I should stay here with you.' She reached for his hand.

'No, you can't. I can see you phoning Eli to tell him you'd decided to stay and him crying, No, Mummy. Come home.'

'You know us Australians,' she said, suddenly desperate. 'We're like boomerangs. We keep on coming back.'

She went into the bedroom to change her clothes. He started to follow her but sat down again instead. He could hear intermittent, familiar sounds, drawers opening and being shut, stretches of silence. It was as if she were packing.

'Are you really leaving on Saturday?' he said.

'What did you say?'

'Saturday. Is that it then?'

'Why don't you come with me?'

'I could never live in a country with no European history. But I'll surprise you one day. I'll ring Eli early and ask what beach you're walking on and I'll just turn up on the sand.'

During that last day, she thought of nothing but Jean-Pierre as she packed and cleaned out her little apartment.

'What do you do, you have a stopover in Dubai?' Jean-Pierre said, standing next to her at the taxi rank in the early morning chill. A bitter wind blew from the mountains. He had come over to carry her bag down the stairs.

'I go straight through. It's three hours on the ground in Dubai, so I walk around the airport then read my book.'

Jean-Pierre looked directly into her eyes. 'I've bought you a little gift,' he said.

'You have?'

'Don't unwrap it until you're on the plane.'

She smiled. 'Okay.' Then she looked at his face, to place him clearly in her mind. He was wearing a white T-shirt and blue jeans under a padded coat. She kissed him on the lips, then got into the taxi.

'Something to take with you,' he said, leaning in the window. In his hand he clasped a small gift-wrapped box. The sun, still low on the horizon, cast an amber glow on his precious face.

'Thank you,' she said. She reached for his hand through the window and then put on her seat belt.

And she thought about this all twenty-four hours of the journey across the Indian Ocean. She would keep opening the little box to admire the marquisite earrings he'd given her. She would catch a taxi from the airport and at home notice the house smelt musty; she would open all the doors and windows to let the air move through, the curtains blowing and air coming in and out. From a far away place, and at night, he would ring to say, resignedly, 'My mother is living with me now.' His gift, when she'd take the earrings out of their black box, would remind her of something that had happened to her once.

She felt like someone who she had always known, that old friend of herself, grounded in home, decisions already made, and behind her somewhere, like the shadow of an identical twin, her other self, who must remain in the far-off distance, never to be exposed to the light.

At the Festival

It was six o'clock in the evening when she finally passed the wind turbines. There, at last, stood Lake George, where long-woolled sheep grazed the field and to the west the Brindabella mountain range was coloured grey and pink by the setting sun. On she drove along an ink-black strip of road where, on either side, tall green-grey eucalypts had formed a welcoming archway. The way flattened out then curved into a narrow empty road. Not one person did she see, not one building, just a handful of brown-bellied cows and later a group of kangaroos standing formidable and still in the headlights. The turn for Watson wasn't clearly signposted but she felt confident in turning east along the row of liquidambars in autumn bloom that took her to the cabins.

Twice on the journey she had pulled into a service station and shut her eyes and briefly rested but now, as she neared Canberra, she felt wide awake and full of energy. Even the dark length of road which progressed flatly to Reception seemed to hold the promise of a new beginning. She sensed the towering, protective presence of the mountain range, the forested hills and, further on, just past the turnoff, the clear, pleasant thump of music coming from the festival.

The receptionist gave her a key, and eagerly she drove further on to cabin number five. Inside, the room was renovated: the two single beds replaced by a double. The same compact kitchenette set into one end of the room but a new television secured to the wall by a multidirectional wall bracket. In between, on the bare linoleum floor, stood a small table laminated with melamine and two matching chairs.

She set her keys and mobile on the table and reached for the electric jug for tea.

After filling the kettle with water from the handbasin in the bathroom, she pressed the remote to turn on the heating, then threw the slippery embroidered cushions from the bed into a corner of the room. Just between the curtains the row of early winter azaleas was quivering brightly under the security lights. She showered, lay down and reached for her Kindle and read the first page of a Katherine Mansfield story. It seemed like an engrossing tale but when she reached the end of the page she felt her eyelids closing, and reluctantly she turned out the light, although she knew that she had all day tomorrow, to work, to read and to walk along the Federal Highway to the festival.

When she woke, she grabbed at the tail of a flimsy dream – a feeling, like a wisp of gossamer – dissipating like the touch of a soap bubble; her sleep had been short and annoyingly elusive. She turned the kettle on and hung her clothes on the wooden hangers on the rack. She had brought little: a Kindle downloaded with books, a small esky of groceries. There was the laptop and several creased bits of paper on which notes were written with arrows and numbered inserts in between the typed paragraphs.

The sky was a calm blue lined with clouds. Up at the festival the poets' breakfast would be underway already. She felt impatient to get there to collect her wristband and program, although she also felt she could lie there on the big bed for days, reading and working, seeing no one. She was thinking about her work, and wondering how she would begin when her mobile alerted her to a text message. For several minutes, the woman sat there not looking at the phone. She reached out not so much to read the message as to move past this distraction.

There was a vacancy after all for the poetry workshop.

When she put the phone down, she turned on the heater again and returned to the Mansfield story. It had no plot or tight dramatic structure. The story followed a character as she prepared to hold a dinner party, sharing her anticipation and her disillusionment when things didn't quite go to plan. At the end of the evening she realises her husband is having an affair.

Something about this story now put the woman in mind of how she had been at another point in her life, when she was contemplating moving in with a man who said he wanted her to live with him, a man she loved, but who had never said he loved her, as though the saying of it would bind him to her, or hide the fact that he didn't.

Once, when she was getting ready for bed, she had stood at the mirror in her cotton nightgown brushing her hair and had sensed him watching her from behind. She was fatter then, and in her forties. He didn't say anything but she sensed he didn't like the look of her at that moment. Perhaps it was the practical night wear he didn't like; or was it that he'd prefer her to wear something more seductive, briefer, more enticing?

She thought of him now as she looked out the window to the azaleas.

'If you move in, I would not want you to make a claim on my money,' he had said. 'I want what I have to go to my children.'

His family, she had known, would always come first.

Now she felt a strong urge to write but told herself it was not something she could do, because she needed to get to the workshop on time. She would just be warming up when she would have to leave and the telling of the story would be interrupted and she would have to put her pen down. She did not like stopping once she was under way.

She cleaned up the breakfast dishes then hurried up the road by the liquidambars to the Federal Highway. The path beside the road was overhung with trees. She put her hand on top of her head to protect herself from swooping birds.

When she found the workshop venue, she sat on a chair by the wall with the others as the last session packed up their musical instruments and left. When the poetry tutor set up at a table, they pulled their chairs around. She was a short middle-aged woman in a spotted dress and woollen cardigan.

'Welcome, everyone,' she said, handing out pieces of paper and blocks of ruled pages for those who needed them. 'Move your chairs in closer. We're only a small group.'

The tutor spoke to them about syllables, matching metre, the rhythm of poems. 'You can get inspiration for your poems anywhere,' she said. 'A news report on the radio. A conversation with someone. Some people need a quiet place to write, and others can work in front of the television.'

*

She hadn't really noticed him at the workshop; he must have been one of the people who had hung back, didn't move their chairs in. But when she saw him again, outside the big marquee where the Bush Poets vs All Other Kinds of Poets debate was about to begin, she recognised his face.

He walked up to her and smiled hello. 'Do you write much poetry?' His tone indicated he was respectful of people who devoted themselves to the written word.

'A little,' she said. 'And you? Do you write?'

'No, no,' he said dismissively. 'But I like going to poetry readings.'

At the end of the session in the marquee, when she saw him waiting in the aisle on the other side of the big tent, she rose from her seat and moved slowly across the fake grass floor in his direction. He stood there as she progressed to the exit until their paths crossed. His hair was thick and white and across his back, secured by thick straps, hung a slim and contoured cyclists' backpack.

'Hello again,' she said.

'Feel like a coffee?' he asked.

'Sounds good to me,' she nodded.

'Which place do you like to go to here?'

'Whichever one has the shortest queue.'

'Let's try next door then.'

He stood in line to order their coffees and suggested she find somewhere for them to sit. 'How about a slice of cake to share?' he said. 'They bake some good tucker here.' He pointed to the end of the counter. 'What about that coconut cake?'

'Looks nice.'

He brought over the drinks and the cake and placed them on the table between them. He used a plastic spoon to cut the slice in half.

I don't usually eat sugary things like this, she reminded herself. But it wasn't something she'd expected, to be sitting here with a man.

He began telling her about his experiences at the yearly festival and how he liked coming each day to the poets' breakfast the best to listen to people recite poems and tell long yarns. He'd been a regular since the death of his wife.

'Why don't you meet me here tomorrow?' he said.

'The breakfast is a bit early for me,' she said. 'But I'll try and get myself up here in time.' She wondered at that moment if she should be interrupting her morning work routine to join him. She would feel obliged to proceed in that direction rather than in the direction of where the work might take her.

*

Back at the cabin, she made herself a light dinner of tuna and avocado on toast, and ate at the table. When the dishes were rinsed and put away, she turned on the heater and lay on the bed and saw again the woman in the Katherine Mansfield story and the blissful happiness this character had felt preparing to spend the evening with friends who were soon to arrive for a dinner party. Is she blissfully happy because she is in denial about her husband's affair? Or is she simply happy without that subconscious knowledge of betrayal? She took up her Kindle and began to closely read every last sentence again. As it turned out, the woman, on finding out about her husband's affair, resigns herself to a life of loneliness.

She lay back and looked through the window and thought about the man with the backpack. Beyond the window was a darkening sky, and a thickly forested hill.

'I am fifty-five years old,' she said, her voice sounding stupid and shrill in the austere room.

*

The next morning, she got up early, showered and dressed quickly. She looked at herself in the mirror, brushed her hair until it shone, then picked up her jacket and walked back along the road to the festival gates. Out over the hills, a thick mist wound its way between the peaks, a soft belt of white embracing the contours of the valley. The shuttle bus that would travel from the main ticket office to the entertainment zone was waiting.

'Slam the door behind you, love,' said the driver when she climbed in.

As the bus circled the main campground, she looked out at the people still asleep in their cars and vans, some in the pre-erected Rent-a-Tents, others under canvas beside their cars, their washing strung up on the support ropes: towels, T-shirts, shorts.

The woman beside her pointed out the window. 'Look. There are the smalls,' she laughed.

It was cold when she stepped off the bus. Never had she seen the place so quiet, so empty of people and music, the grassed areas and the wide gravel avenues all deserted, although the food stalls were opening their shutters. She wondered what time the place would come to life again and where she could get a hot drink.

The thing was, she really should be back at the cabin working at her desk. She could quickly walk to one of the gates, hop on a shuttle bus and return to the room. Instead, she stopped at one of the rectangular water stations to fill her paraben-free bottle. A volunteer, in distinguishing bright yellow vest, was using a hose to refill the dispenser.

'Is it plain tap water?' she asked.

'Clean Canberra water,' he said proudly.

'The same as in the Ladies?'

'Yes. Pure water, but a better atmosphere.'

She laughed, then looked around and saw a bearded man in moleskins, singlet top and akubra hat boiling water in huge vats over a roaring fire. Awkwardly, she stepped over the logs to a table set up with billy tea and toasted damper for sale.

She sat there at the fire and kicked at the earth beneath her feet as the golden line of the sunrise made its way above the line of trees. She found herself relaxing into the moment as warmth spread down and over her face and neck and into her shoulders. This, she said to herself, is where she should be, at this moment, in her life.

On the branch of a tree, a large-beaked bird purposefully surveyed the terrain, his head moving rapidly from left to right before he hopped to another branch. He was not a pretty bird, ink-black feathers, and what looked like a white mask circling his eyes, as if he'd donned a Zorro cape before he'd flown out of the house. He flew down to the edge of the gravel path where it merged with the grass, oblivious to the pigeons already scratching in the dust. He pecked at the road, then stopped, loosened his wings, and swooped back up to his eyrie in the tree.

Sitting there, watching the bird do battle with the pigeons for tiny treasures, she'd thought of her work. The mug of tea was hot and satisfying, the treacle spread thickly on the damper. While she savoured the smoky bread and the sweet orange-coloured tea, a part of her mind was also preoccupied with meeting up again with the man with the backpack. She wondered, for a moment, what colour his eyes were, exactly how tall was he? Tall, but how tall?

At eight-thirty she walked down the path past the circus tent towards the poets' breakfast marquee. She paused at the entry, looking for him. She stood there a moment then made her way to sit down beside him.

*

On the Sunday, after a week of spending each day together at the festival, attending events and sharing stories of their lives over coffees and cake and beers and takeaway meals, she couldn't see him at their usual meeting place, so waited just outside the tent. When she glanced around and saw the back of a tall man with a contoured backpack enter the marquee, accompanied by a woman, she wasn't sure if it was him at first. She waited in a spot where she couldn't be seen as they sat down side by side. She watched as the woman took a health bar out of her handbag, bite into it, then give him the other half. Her hand rested on his thigh.

So he wasn't single after all. What a stupid mistake she'd made. She stood there watching the two of them, feeling angry, with him and with herself. Had she learnt nothing? A woman of her age. What had she expected? What had she wanted from this man?

It was late when she returned to the cabin. A whole week had passed her by but there she found herself, back at the desk, looking out at the hedge of azaleas. There was a highway out there, a mountain range and forested hills standing erect and dignified. She thought of the Katherine Mansfield character, Bertha, who was deceived by her husband. She thought of the tall man and how he'd divided the slice of cake to share with her that first day, and began to imagine the life he must have with the woman. There was a power point located under the table; she plugged her laptop in and turned it on. Not until she typed in her password and heard the 'ready' chime did she realise she was struggling to control the shaking of her fingers over the keyboard.

Canberra Folk Festival, she typed, and the date. She thought of the woman's hand on the man's thigh, and for no reason her breath caught in her chest. She wanted to say what it was like when he'd introduced his partner and how he'd invited her to join them for coffee.

'This is Elaine,' he'd said. 'She had nothing to do today.' He'd said the words with apology in his tone. Was it an apology?

She'd stood in line beside him to place their coffee order and had insisted on paying her own way this time. Elaine waited at the table. When they'd returned with the drinks, she'd noticed Elaine had removed the man's small cyclist's bag from the chair between them and relocated him beside herself at the end.

And then Elaine's questioning. Why have you come all this way? Where are your friends? You did come to the festival with friends, didn't you?

Several times as she typed, she thought of the Bertha character who'd resigned herself to a life of loneliness. At one point she stopped and looked at the moon's position in the sky. When she glanced up again, the moon was concealed behind a thick layer of cloud. By this time, her central character was following part of the Tour de France route on his new lightweight bicycle. She went over the paragraph where his bike strikes a kerb near Chamonix in the French Alps, his body limp and unconscious on the road, and realised her back was aching. When she got up, she felt stiff but satisfied. She looked out at the moonlight now hitting the hedge of azaleas and anticipated a good night's sleep. As she turned the kettle on, she lengthened her spine and was planning his months ahead in the Geneva hospital, and his slow and very painful road to recovery.

Aunt Helen

Although she loved her nieces and nephews, it was when she turned thirty-nine that driving young children around in her car seemed to make her nervous – precious cargo is how the grandparents described it – a tightening in the stomach. 'Aunty Helen, would you like to take Naomi to see the Muppets? Are you free?' Always these requests from one of her sisters looking tired and desperate – one of her younger siblings, they used to be so close – and Helen would force herself to make the effort to be the good aunty. The responsibility of passengers in her car always made her anxious. She was anxious about one thing or the other most of the time, but wanted to appear selfless and generous-spirited. Her availability, or non-availability, was noted, itemised, either in her favour, or against her. She didn't want to be labelled self-obsessed. She had entered an era when the nicest thing a person could say to her was, 'You're a fabulous aunty. The kids love you.'

It was when she was sitting at home watching telly one Sunday night that Leah had rung to ask about taking Naomi to the movies in the holidays. Helen drove over to pick the little girl up before Leah left for work, secured the child into the seat belt carefully, babbling away all the time, enthusiastically, 'Lovely to see you, gorgeous girl. You look so pretty. I love the sparkly shoes and the sparkles on your top.'

Naomi smiled with pride, touching the golden wings of the butterfly embroidered on her T-shirt.

Helen indicated before pulling away from the kerb into the outside lane, at the same time turning the radio off and the air con on, before stopping at a red light. She had glanced in the rear-vision mirror and, amid the sounds of engines idling and a bus changing gears, saw a truck moving up quickly behind her – he won't be able to stop in time – swerving to the inside lane and heading too close to the passenger side of the car where Naomi was sitting – the truck, the great big truck, was about to crash into the car! And when she felt the thrust of the impact cricking her neck – in the slow motion of the crunch of metal, she saw the other stationary cars at the lights, the wind flipping between the fronds of the pavement palms and one fluffy cloud like a giant arm reaching out across the sky. After Naomi was rushed to Westmead Hospital with head and limb injuries and after surgery and the police interviews, Helen slowly returned home.

She refused to leave her top-floor apartment, and there was much worrying for her, on the part of all the family, including Leah, who wrote a long and detailed letter to tell Helen that it wasn't her fault.

Damion usually skyped her from London each week; he had become her most loyal and supportive friend. He was semi-retired after working as an economist, though he looked more like an English version of Crocodile Dundee – deep character lines carved into his face, wide white smile, shark-tooth necklace, a favourite khaki shirt and many-pocketed hiking trousers. They'd met years ago on a walking trip in the Ardeche and she'd stayed in his spare room many times when visiting London. He was getting ready to return home after a month on the French Riviera. He'd rented an apartment in a small fishing village by the sea near Monaco.

'You could have this place for a month early winter,' he suggested. 'Jacqueline offers a very cheap deal in the off-season. It would do you good.' He told Helen she could use the time to work on one of her special projects. 'You can read and write, go for long walks. Or not. Trains and buses at the doorstep.'

She looked into his face on the monitor, warily, then lowered her gaze. She still felt timid and shaky. 'I don't know,' she said. She had spent a good part of the year lying around in her yoga gear and thick woollen socks in front of the heater, taking in the morning sun through the north-facing window, her hair a knotted mess, a bird's nest, but no baby bird. She felt claustrophobic and unsteady. 'The hardest part would be getting myself into a taxi and out to the airport.'

She watched closely as a buzzing fly kept doing kamikaze dives around the room and then throwing itself at the glass of the window.

'If I decide to go, would you come for a visit?'

'Of course I would. We're old friends.' He was a down-to-earth man. When she had been staying at his place once, and been dumped by an American she met in Spain, Damion sat her down in his kitchen with a glass of Pernod. 'Let's look at this logically,' he said.

She wished he was with her now, offering her another glass of Pernod.

'I don't think, Damion, that I can get myself out of here.'

'Of course you can.' He reached up to his head and smoothed his hair back over the shiny expanse of his forehead.

'Getting through the days is as much as I can manage,' she said. 'Making plans is beyond me.' She didn't know what else to say to him. But she smiled all the same. Didn't want to appear a chronic depressive. Didn't want him to worry about her.

'Keep it simple,' he encouraged. 'Fly directly from Sydney to Nice.' He smiled his big toothy grin back at her. '"Just say to yourself, "What's the worst thing that could happen?"' He told her the apartment block in the Old Town was right on the water. She'd be able to see fish swimming in the Mediterranean from her balcony.

At least if she left Sydney she wouldn't be responsible for the death of any more of her nieces or nephews.

She was met at the airport by Jacqueline, her bilingual landlady, who held up a large card with her name on it, and when Helen walked towards her, she nodded and said, 'Hi, bonjour, Madame Hayes?'

The drive to Villefranche sur Mer took half an hour, around the curve of the Promenades des Anglais, through Nice and along the Base

Corniche, but it wasn't until Jacqueline pulled up at the top of the cliff-like hillside laden with beautiful gardens and stunning villas that Helen could see the Old Town cascading down to the sea, and when Jacqueline led the way down the stone steps, it wasn't until then, it occurred to Helen that it was thanks to Damion's help she was able to dig herself out of the warm nest of home. She'd managed to get here.

Jacqueline stopped at a dark yellow thirteenth-century building on the waterfront quay. She showed Helen the stone arches next to the building supporting the pedestrian path leading to the beach and the train station. She pointed up to the top floor before unlocking the door and leading the way up the stairs. Another door opened into the elegant and spacious main living area – lounge room, dining, well-stocked kitchen – and an office with a desk. There were two armchairs, reading lights and a big sofa. Yellow walls, old terracotta tiles on the floors, oriental carpets.

'What do you think?' Jacqueline asked.

'Wow. It's amazing,' she said, walking out through the French doors to a long, wrap-around balcony. She could see boats bobbing on the turquoise harbour and people walking along the quay. A huge view of the bay. I'll work on the terrace when the weather is fine, she thought, and patted her laptop in its bag on her shoulder that contained the first chapter of *Death on the Sydney Harbour Bridge*.

'You'll be able to listen to the sounds of the sea all night,' said Jacqueline, ushering Helen towards the master bedroom.

The room was tasteful and cosy – bedside lights, a queen-size bed, a window overlooking the Place du Conseil, a triangular-shaped square with wrought-iron street lamps and a fountain, and beside it, the famous Chapel of Saint Pierre with its murals painted by Jean Cocteau.

There was a cleaner once a week, said Jacqueline. There were office supplies, wifi, international calling and Sky TV with English channels. A weekly soirée for all the tenants. Welcome aperitifs at six in the bar below.

Helen felt totally exhausted. When Jacqueline handed over the keys and departed, Helen threw herself on the bed, wrapped herself around a pillow, scrunching her hands up like cat's paws beside her sleep-creased cheek, and then slept until six, dreaming that she was together with a child on a boat, but the child stepped off the back of the boat onto a wharf without Helen noticing and she'd inadvertently sailed away leaving the little girl behind.

A loud sound woke her up – a knocking on the door. It was time to meet for drinks downstairs. She rolled slowly to the side of the bed, sat there for a few minutes, then stood up. Unpacking took only a few minutes. Cautiously, she left the bulk of her clothes in her bag, telling herself that she could get out of here and catch a plane home whenever she wanted, although knowing that everything would probably stay where it was and be a crushed mess just when she needed something nice to wear. What the hell? Who cared? She took her toiletries into the bathroom and showered before putting on a pleated dress, which, because she hadn't worn it for such a long time, she had forgotten how much it billowed in a formless shape from her shoulders. You could be pregnant under there, she said to her reflection in the mirror before retrieving bag and key and making her way to the stairs.

She pulled her stomach in and squared her shoulders but couldn't make the dress flatten at the front. She should have brought a belt. Maybe she should go inside and hop back into bed. But, no, who cared what she looked like? She wasn't there to impress anyone.

A pale light filtered through a large window over the stairwell. She took a deep breath and held firmly to the railing. Through a door at the bottom of the stairs she could hear restrained laughter – was it laughter? Yes! It was laughter – echoing from the salon where she supposed champagne to be in progress, and then, as she got closer, a sudden insistent yapping. Oh, no, not a noisy dog to put up with. At the foot of the stairs crouched a small white poodle with a tangerine diamond-studded collar, whose barking turned to a baby-like whimpering until a red-haired woman, with cat's eye glasses in a matching tangerine colour, rushed out of the salon, gathered the dog into her arms and covered him with kisses.

'Louis, Louis, my darling.'

The dog looked up at her. 'That's love,' the woman said to no one in particular. 'See how he looks at me?'

How interesting, thought Helen.

At a small upright piano an elderly woman with shoulder-length white ringlets was playing heart-wrenching melodies from the era of Edith Piaf. 'I own every song Piaf ever sang,' Damion, the Francophile, had said once.

Jacqueline was helping out behind the bar at the opposite end of the salon mixing Kir Royale aperitifs. 'Come in, Helen,' she called out. 'Welcome,' she said, handing Helen what looked like a flute of red cordial.

Helen looked around to see who else was there. The room was pretty empty. Well, what did you expect at this time of the year? she said to herself. This slowly darkening time when the tourists had left and the hotels and restaurants were preparing to close for the winter. But she reminded herself that this was an excellent opportunity to finish a draft of *Death on the Sydney Harbour Bridge*.

The dog lady was sitting with a youngish woman – who must be her younger sister, a slimmer version with thicker, paler, longer hair – and a red-haired child. Both women watched as the young girl clicked her multicoloured pen and drew on a small notepad.

The younger woman, who must be the child's mother, looked down at the drawing. 'It looks like a spider's web,' she said.

'It is, Mummy. A square spider's web.'

'You could put a spider in the web and a bug,' her mother suggested.

The child nodded and kept on drawing. 'I am,' she said. 'Here's a mummy spider and here's a baby spider.' The little girl slowly and carefully pulled the page out of the spiral notebook then inspected the paper beneath. 'Look,' she said, running her finger over the indentations on the page, like a blind person reading braille, 'It's found the pattern.'

'Yes,' her mother said. 'Amazing.'

The child looked up when a note of over-the-top glamour entered the salon; a woman, probably the same age as her mother, her hair caught up in a bun with a flower securing it in place, her shoes an unusual geometric-patterned extremely high wedge, her stretch fabric dress just covering her bottom as she walked to the bar.

The child clicked her pen, changing the colour from pink to purple. 'She's fancy,' she said.

'Fancy?' said the woman with the dog, who must be the aunty.

'She's fancy-pantsy,' said the child. 'She looks cool and fancy and pretty.' She smiled at her mother, seeking approval for her summation of the colourful woman.

Helen felt a pang of envy for the vibrant family group, so alive, so at ease with each other, so loving and encouraging to the child. As long as they were all together, they'd be happy anywhere. Thinking about them brought back painful memories. There was love there, between mother and child, and laughter, and physical contact, none of which she had ever known. Her cold Russian mother, Svetlana, was an unstable delicate woman, a former beauty whom Father idolised. Father didn't have enough love to go around. His wife was his world. Neither Mother nor Father really knew their three little girls. Helen remembered the dread in the pit of her stomach when Father returned from the surgery and she'd hear his key in the door, 'What did you do to upset your mother today?' he'd shout at Helen. He blamed Helen for everything. Mother's illness, her heart attack, everything. When Mother died at forty-eight, Father wept like a baby, but then, within the year, he'd remarried.

When the two women and the child decided to make a move, Helen was pleased when the aunty, carrying Louis in her arms, turned and gave her a little smile of greeting before they left the room. She watched the sisters and the child lovingly entwined as they walked to the door.

Then there was nothing for her to do but go for a walk.

Through the iron door, across the deserted road, and along the shore of the beach she walked in the fading light of that blue day. The stillness engulfed her once she was past the end of the beach. The water was almost stationary; tiny waves, a solitary lamp gleamed above her, turning the sharp leaves of a pine tree into a dagger.

No sound of screaming brakes in this place, just the sound of her own steps as she walked back across the gravel, along the sand, and over the small pebbles.

'If this apartment wasn't smack bang on the water, I'd leave now,' she Skyped to Damion.

'As soon as you make a start on one of your projects, you'll feel better,' he said.

She was sitting up in bed, her computer on her knees. It could be forever before she wrote another paragraph. 'There's hardly a soul in sight,' she said in a whiny voice. She hated it when she caught herself complaining like that. Just concentrate on the positives, she reminded herself.

'If you could get the final instalment of the Parker Powell series completed, Harper Collins would jump for joy,' said Damion in an encouraging voice.

'I'm going to check on flights out of here,' insisted Helen.

'Don't be silly,' he said, his forehead crinkling into a scowl. He widened his eyes at her.

Maybe he was right; she should just get back to work and she'd feel much better. 'Probably too hard to get another booking with everyone travelling for Christmas,' she murmured.

'And twice the price for the airfare,' he said, folding his arms in front of his chest and leaving them there, like a barrier, like a fortress. And then began softly to sing 'La Marseillaise'.

Next morning, a cold wind blew across the mountains. Helen awoke to the sound of rattling windows. Sitting up slowly in the alien bed, she

squinted at the bedside clock. She had assumed it was her usual –
awake at just past dawn and in the grip of anxiety – but she saw to her
surprise that it was nearly eight-thirty, and a weak strip of light
appearing at the base of the blind seemed to signal a dull day. She
rolled out of bed and pulled the blind up; in her thick bed socks and
flannelette pyjamas, she stepped out onto the terrace and shivered in
the icy air. A mist had descended on the sea, and ahead of her in the far
distance she had trouble making out the white mansions and dark
green vegetation of the Cap Ferrat peninsula. Below her, two small
boats bobbed on the harbour, fishing nets neatly stacked, a man hosing
down the decks.

She dressed slowly, layer on layer, adding a down coat at the last,
after the matching down vest and, opening the doors to the terrace
again, she went out and set her laptop on the table. The bracing air
would force her back to some semblance of life. She breathed in deeply
before beginning a morning of imaginings.

She pulled out her notebook to draft a scene of a woman being hit
by a van as she stepped out on a pedestrian crossing. The driver of the
florist's van must have run an amber light. But later, after the hospital,
and during the police interview, the courier denied he'd run an amber
or a red light. To the woman's family, it was obvious that the driver
hadn't wanted to stop suddenly with his van full of flowers. He'd be up
for replacement costs. The woman told the paramedics that of course
she'd waited for the little green man to appear. She'd never cross on a
red light at a pedestrian crossing, it wasn't in her personality. In the
ambulance, they'd had to cut off her beautiful Italian leather boots to
free her crushed limbs.

At the hospital, the orthopaedic emergency doctor inserted a steel
rod in her leg and two screws at the ankle. The woman reckoned the
doctor said that the sight of her foot, hanging by skin only, had made
him feel sick. Who would believe a surgeon would say something like
that?

'Does it sound true that an emergency doctor would say to a patient that the sight of her injuries made him feel ill?' she asked Damion on Skype.

He stood up to turn the volume down on Barbara Streisand, then sat back in front of the screen. 'No,' he said, frowning. 'Seems inappropriate. Why?'

'That's what my sister said.'

'How so?' He looked at her narrowly.

'At the hospital. After the accident. That's what the emergency doctor said when they brought Naomi in. That's what Leah says when she tells the story of what happened.'

'At least she's able to speak about it now.'

'Yes,' Helen said defensively. 'Apparently, she keeps on talking about it. Telling that same story about what the surgeon said before he operated.'

She began in the afternoons, after staggering out of her room, dazed and exhausted from several hours with *Death on the Sydney Harbour Bridge*, to go for a walk.

Dressed in black jeans tucked into furry après ski boots and the long down coat, she made her way up the stairs behind the apartment block to a small plaza where two men played boules, watched by four silent onlookers. She walked on until she came to a large café, behind whose glass windows three chandeliers twinkled. She went in and sat down, taking a notebook out of her bag to give herself a prop. Such a relief that the door was kept firmly shut from the wind. Loaves of thick, crusty bread filled straw baskets, the usual croissants, pastries, Florentines and pastel-coloured macaroons.

The coffee, in a fine porcelain cup with antique silver spoon on the saucer, was brought to the table by a waiter in a white shirt, velvet bow tie and circular gaping holes in his earlobes. She wondered if he'd had the giant empty holes punched into his lobes or had his skin stretched out over time.

In the far corner she could see the two sisters and the red-haired child. The child looked about the same age as Naomi. Would have been the same age as Naomi, if Helen hadn't been in such a rush that day to get to the yoga class. If only Helen hadn't been so selfish, Naomi would still be alive. Watching the red-headed child yet again, she felt the ache in her gut that preceded tears.

She sipped the coffee. It was hot, but bitter.

The little girl was eating a mauve macaroon with a filling that left bits of purple stain on the corners of her mouth. Louis waited under her chair for any crumbs to drop from the table.

'Guess what?' the girl said to her aunty.

'What?'

'I've got four wiggly teeth.'

'Really! Which ones?'

The girl opened her mouth and pointed with the tip of her finger.

'I hope they don't all fall out at once, or you won't be able to eat.'

'I've got plenty of other teeth,' the little girl laughed.

Helen turned her attention to Louis Armstrong's voice in the background as he sang, 'When you kiss me…when you press me to your heart…'

Just then, her thoughts were interrupted by a friendly male voice saying, '*Un autre café crème?*'

Startled, she looked up to see the waiter with the hollow rings in his ears poised with pen and notepad. She murmured, 'Non, merci,' expecting him to move away; she could hardly invite him to sit down and join her.

'*Australienne?*' he enquired, in a voice that was slightly flirtatious in its lilting upward inflection.

At least he didn't think she was English. She gave a distracted smile, intending to discourage him from asking any more questions, but changed her mind and asked him instead about his earrings.

He told her it had taken a long time for his ear lobes to stretch. 'I make since I was fifteen,' he said. 'Very painful. You like?'

'Yes, they look good,' she said.

He walked away towards the kitchen, far from the café tables and out into another place. She could hear laughter that was perceptible, even across the width of the café from the direction of the kitchen.

'*Ça va?*' Skyped Damion.

She watched as he realigned his bushy eyebrows with a lick of his finger.

'*Comme ci, comme ça,*' she said. 'Some of the faces are becoming familiar.'

'How did the weekend go?'

She waved her hands in the air in front of her face, like a pair of windscreen wipers, and shook her head. 'I got through it.'

'You made it to Monday?'

'Yes. Exactly. I made it to Monday,' she said.

Damion laughed his big laugh. She looked at him. This week, she said, she would attempt to walk to Eze Village to check out the ancient ruins and the cactus gardens.

'A long way to climb up to Eze,' he warned. 'Very, very steep. You can catch a bus, you know.'

'I need some strenuous exercise or I'll go crazy here.'

The next evening, she told herself she must make the effort to go to the weekly soirée in the downstairs bar. After all, Jacqueline had organised it especially. She showered and dressed and found a pair of tiger-skin stilettos to strap to her ankles. She'd never have the refined elegance of a French woman, but she would do her best to make her legs look French.

Downstairs in the salon, the pianist, sitting down to play, gave her a brief nod. She nodded back and thought how limited her means of communication had become. She gave herself a talking to, said she must try harder, do better than that. So with determination in her stride she sat down at the bar next to the tall slim beauty with the tiny stretch miniskirt and the gigantic wedge shoes who told her, without any questioning, that she'd enrolled at the local French language school.

'French lessons?' said Helen. 'Great idea. I'm hopeless at languages.'

'You just have to be game enough to open your mouth and try,' said the woman with a smile. 'I've tried for years,' she added. 'Tried really hard. But sometimes the waiters still don't seem to realise I'm speaking French when I place my order.'

'How awful for you.'

'I suppose it's my American accent.'

Her name was Meredith Nike and she holidayed in Villefranche every year. Her dark hair was pulled tightly back into a ponytail – an instant facelift, she'd joked – her skin smooth and unlined, her lips full and luscious, her teeth as white and regular as a piano's keys.

She asked Helen if she'd like to walk into Nice with her the next day. It would take an hour or so.

They met near the train station, Meredith dressed all in white with matching pristine joggers, and then they headed out, up the steps and towards the Parc du Mont Boron.

'It's so charming here, isn't it?' said Meredith.

Down along the sidewalk beside the main road were stunning views of the sea, the mountains in the background not yet tipped with snow. It was December and they were reaching up to the clouds as if praying for a white Christmas. The air was crisp. An antidote to lethargy.

Helen sighed. 'It's a popular place for retirees. Do you think any-one has any adventures here?'

Meredith smiled. 'You're right. The people our age, and younger, seem to have moved to the cities.'

Helen wondered if Meredith was single. Such an attractive woman. 'Are you married?' she asked.

Meredith gave a cynical chuckle. 'No. I haven't met the right man yet. What about you?'

'Briefly. I'm not much good at relationships. My father used to say to me, "You change your men like you change your underwear."'

Meredith laughed before stopping to tighten her laces. 'Who is good at relationships?' She paused before asking, 'Do you have any children?'

'No. I've never wanted to have a child. Never yearned to be a mother. Never felt I was missing out on anything. And, anyway, I have my sisters' children. I love them like my own. I just get irritated when I have to help out too often and feel I can't say no.'

Everything about Meredith seemed larger than life: her height, the length of her extraordinary legs, her guttural voice, her huge emerald-coloured eyes. I must be careful, thought Helen. I'm not going to confide anything about the accident to this glamorous and gorgeous woman. She'd probably be horrified.

They walked on in silence as they climbed the steps from the coast road stopping at the ancient ruins where they could see the arch of the beach of Nice below, and the amphitheatre of hills in the background.

'Look, there's someone parasailing,' said Meredith pointing out to the water.

They continued, past the bend in the road on the Boulevard Princess Grace, where they looked at the concrete memorial to Grace Kelly.

'This must be near where her car left the road,' said Helen. 'A hairpin bend. They say it was a mother/daughter moment with out-of-control Stephanie.'

Meredith nodded. 'Sometimes there's very little to stop a vehicle veering over the cliff edge.'

Sleep did not come easily that night. She was a beautiful little girl. A really beautiful child, both inside and out. Helen shivered and wrapped her arms around herself. She lay awake searching for an image of Naomi, listening for the sound of her voice but she could see and hear nothing.

And here was Helen in Villefranche, when she should be at home giving support to Leah over the difficult period of Christmas and New Year. She was the eldest, after all. The big sister. Hold their hands. Don't let go of their hands. Wait until your sisters get off the bus.

Between disjointed dreams that flashed in Helen's head, she saw a woman being run over by her own car. The woman was trapped underneath the vehicle. She'd walked behind it and somehow the car had rolled over her and crushed her body. Police said that neighbours called emergency services immediately, but when paramedics arrived the woman was pronounced dead.

When Helen woke up, much later than usual, it was with the familiar and deadly knowledge that the day would be a write-off. She took a shower but felt dizzy and disorientated, just like jet lag. She spoke sternly to herself. She knew that depression hovered and must be prevented. Writing was out of the question. Practise kindness and compassion, she counselled herself.

The pulled curtains revealed a bright blue sky with a scattering of clouds. On the pier, an artist had set up his easel. She could see the man's palette knife carving quickly into the paint and across the canvas. The bells of the Chapel of Saint Pierre rang. It must be Sunday.

A plan B, of the kind at which she had become very skilled, was what she needed. Maybe she could allow herself to just lie in the sun on the terrace and read. She felt so tired, a tiredness that ruled out any enthusiasm for anything, any peace of mind, any relaxing into the moment.

The bright day had within it the possibility of a change of direction: it was the beginning of winter after all. Sun burned through the clouds: flowering bougainvillea and violet-coloured irises stood resolute in the weakening light. The trees had lost their abundance and were grieving for the dull brown leaves which lay on the ground beneath them. The only sound now was the clinking of the ships' bells.

Deciding against plan B, she knew that vigorous exercise was what she needed. That's what she'd do. A walk to Eze Village. She packed food and water in a day pack and laced up her hiking boots. She opened the door, walked down the steps, let herself out of her dark cave.

She made her way towards Promenade Maurice Rouvier, where she saw the waiter from the café, dressed today in jeans and black jumper, a book in his hand leaning on the side railing and looking out to sea.

Catching sight of her, he called out, '*Bonjour, madame.*' He asked where she was going.

'To Eze,' she said.

He said he could drive her there. It was a long and difficult uphill walk. Four hundred metres above sea level. His name was Gilles.

She fiddled with the straps of the backpack that dug into her shoulders, feeling self-conscious that he was looking through her clothing. She'd unintentionally put on a black bra beneath the white sweat shirt. 'No thanks,' she said. 'I want to walk.' She gave him a wave goodbye, turned and crossed the road.

After half an hour of strenuous climbing on washed-out paths and over loose stones, she saw Gilles drive up the hill towards her in a small black sedan. Again he offered her a lift.

Perhaps she should have accepted his offer, she thought later. It was all too hot and too far to walk in the end. She'd given up and gone shopping to the supermarket in Beaulieu sur Mer instead.

That's when she'd seen Gilles again.

She was sitting outside at a café surrounded by her white plastic shopping bags. Not a very sexy look. He sat down beside her and ordered a coffee.

'It's good getting out into the sunshine,' she said. 'I've had a good day, even though I didn't make it to Eze.'

Would he think she looked happy now? Less serious? Had her face lost its sadness and become more friendly and open? Would he be wondering what she's doing here in Villefranche?

'Do you live here?' asked Helen.

'No,' he said. He told her he lived in Paris but was staying at his grandmother's house in Beaulieu to earn some extra money in the holidays. 'And you?' he asked. 'Why are you here?'

'I'm working on a book,' said Helen. 'I'm here to read and to write and to go for long walks.'

He took a sip of his coffee, then told her his passion was for poetry and philosophy. 'I was hoping you come with me to the beach to watch the colour of the clouds at sunset,' he said after a pause. 'It is too *beau* to waste.'

Yes, go, Helen said to herself. What the hell? She always did admire persistence.

An unexpected pleasure, she thought, grateful to have a companion, as they walked slowly away from the little village, along the water's edge. The row of pine trees a dark contrast to the shimmer of the sea. Soon the sun would drop behind the hills. The day was very slowly darkening, the blue of the sky fading in that in-between hour which signals the end of the day. The sadness that comes with the approach of night sank heavily into her being.

Gilles glanced at her. 'Will we sit here by the rocks?' he suggested, guiding her to a sandy spot against the sea wall. Taking his shoes off, he asked her if she minded if he lit a cigarette.

Helen shook her head.

He lit up. 'I need to have more life experiences,' he sighed. 'So I have something to write my poems about.'

So that was it, thought Helen. How funny. That's what he wants? Well, it was the same for her. For the first time in forever, she giggled. The sound, so unexpected, surprised her. Once started, the giggling soon turned to laughing. She could not stop laughing.

Gilles looked at her with a puzzled expression as the laughter brought tears to her eyes. Eventually, he laughed too while Helen dabbed at her eyes. She took a deep and steadying breath, then put her arm around him.

He leaned in closer. 'I would like to suggest that I take you out one day soon,' he said. 'Have you been to Saint-Paul-de-Vence?'

She shook her head.

'A medieval city,' he said. 'All the tourists like to go. And there are some nice little restaurants. We can have lunch there.'

They retraced their steps to his car.

That evening, after a drink at the bar, Helen found herself smiling from time to time. She was, actually, pleasantly tired and felt more evenly balanced than usual. When she soaked in a hot bath, and after applying a French body balm, that smelt of Tangerine Rind, Vanille and Sandalwood, she thought, I will sleep well tonight.

'I'm going on an outing with a French waiter tomorrow,' she skyped to Damion. 'His name is Gilles.'

Damion grinned at her. She could hear a Charles Aznavour tape playing in the background. 'I've heard about those French men,' he said.

'You have?'

'You'll have to tell me if it's true or not.'

'Sure, sure. As if!' said Helen waving her hand dismissively. 'He's got a car. That's the attraction.'

She looked out to the bright pink clouds in the darkening sky and watched as the evening light diffused over the honey-coloured walls of the old stone houses.

The next morning, she made her way up the steps and archways of the narrow streets lined with shops selling souvenirs and artisan products: paintings of Villefranche and its deep harbour, hand-painted ceramics, clay and figurines. There'd been a thick mist over the sea and she'd heard on the radio that flights out of Nice had been cancelled. But now the mist had lifted. She kept walking along the winding laneways, covered by the upper storeys of ancient pastel-coloured buildings until, at the top of the final stairs to the main square, she heard the cluck of a mother hen with her chicks in a grassy area of a backyard.

Gilles, dressed in black trousers, charcoal-grey jumper, and cashmere jacket, stepped out to greet her.

'The only life around here seems to be on the pétanque pitch,' said

Helen with disappointment as they watched a group of men play boules.

'Yes,' agreed Gilles. 'Saint-Paul-de-Vence used to be full of artists. You could see them at work. Chagall, he painted here for twenty years. He loved the trees, the amorous couples, the goats and the cockerels flying across the village. We can see his grave.'

They were seated outside a small cafe under a bougainvillea-covered archway, a bottle of chilled Rosé on the table between them. Protected from the glare, they were able to look across the gardens dotted with palm trees, made greener by the brightness of early afternoon. At this height, in the walled city, they could see the olive groves of flowering daises. Up here, the air smelt fresh and invigorating.

'Who comes here?' she asked. 'Apart from the tourists – the day-trippers from the cruise ships.'

He poured her another glass of wine. 'People like you and me.'

Helen leaned back in her chair and smiled.

In her mind, the two sisters, the red-headed child, the bar with its elderly pianist and the apartment's sought-after location, seemed to be part of another world. The morose and lethargic person that she had been in the low-lying basin by the sea, had evaporated on the way to this upper air, after the beautiful drive through the countryside outside Nice and the walk past the art galleries and little shops tucked into the meandering traffic-free streets. By some far-flung and opaque process, new patterns were forming, resulting in something more definitive, more glistening, more substantial, able to appreciate pleasure, even to feel entitled to it.

After lunch, Gilles asked, 'Are you ready to walk up to the ramparts?' and they set off again until they reached the top of the fortress.

A noise from her computer woke her up. It was the familiar boom boom music of Skype calling.

'So how did the date go?' asked Damion.

'It wasn't a date. He drove me to Saint-Paul-de-Vence.'

'Amazing place, isn't it? So…how did the day go?'

'Great. Really great. Very cold up on the ramparts, though. He offered me his coat. A real gentleman.'

'Don't be fooled by that. He probably just wants to get into your knickers.'

'How crass of you, Damion,' she laughed. 'Keep your opinions to yourself and don't spoil things.'

She didn't tell Damion how Gilles had opened his jacket to her up on the parapet and how she'd snuggled in close and heard the rhythm of his heart as he wrapped his coat tightly around her. She'd inhaled the freshly washed smell at his neck and the olive wood scent that rose from the valley below. She felt herself soften into the warmth of him.

Back in her room, she'd sat down to wait for Gilles.

When he came, as she knew he would, one or two hours later, they said nothing but looked at each other with the ache of desire.

He frowned when she tried to lead him into the bedroom and asked what was the rush. Didn't she know that's not how a French man made love. 'French men love women,' he said. 'We have all the night, *ma cherie*.'

Later, she lay on the bed in her satin nightgown, which had not been torn but was pulled off her shoulders and twisted up around her. Gilles was kissing her mouth, lips, nose, cheeks, ears, eyes and forehead. The room was brimming with gratefulness and indulgence, a rich potage of love and lust. She traced with her fingers the curves and angles of the webbed pattern of his biceps tattoo, just like the red-headed child had done in the café when she'd retraced the lines of her spiderweb drawing.

Then suddenly she rolled over to the edge of the bed and curled around a pillow, her hair covering her face. She'd begun to cry.

'*Ma petite*,' he soothed. He pushed the hair away from her eyes.

'A child died because of me,' she murmured.

'*Merde!*'

'A car accident.'

Gilles wiped her wet cheeks, then kissed her eyelids closed. '*Ma cherie*,' he was saying.

She felt far away, as if she were back home, walking through the neighbourhood and looking in the lighted windows at the weekend parties, the family dinners. She'd breathe in the smell of food cooking. Borscht? Was it the same as her mother used to make? The thing was, she could forgive her Russian mother. She'd come to that realisation on the day her mother died. She understood that Mother had done the best that she could – with her limitations. But Father? He should have known better.

She turned away, towards the window. No, she'd never forgive Father. But could she forgive herself?

Above the spiral of the chapel, where the mist had lifted, she thought she saw a plane. She turned, and for a moment it seemed they were all there behind the window of the aircraft, all the random car victims, all the faces of the mothers and the children, and the spirit of the dead child telling her it was okay, it wasn't her fault.

There was a moon, she noticed, opening the thick curtains and stepping out on to the terrace, and the air was fresh and new. She sat for a time, turning many thoughts over in her mind. A beautiful night, lovely, peaceful. More peaceful than most.

Back in bed, with Gilles' arms wrapped around her, in that moment just before sleep, she became aware of a softness in her limbs – realised how rigidly she'd been holding herself – and of how much safety was available, here, in this moment, in the embrace of this man.

It was her last day in Villefranche. She stepped again through the iron door into a late afternoon of such tranquil beauty that she wondered how she could possibly have missed it. A winter sunset, soft like a peach, gilded the clouds; tiny waves sighed into the sand of the beach; a huge cruise ship passed noiselessly off in the direction of Nice; and at her feet, on the pebbly path, she saw the flicker of a lizard as it made its escape – in less than a heartbeat – through a gap in what looked to be an impenetrable brick wall.

Towards the End

He leaned back on the chrome chair, stretched his legs out under the square black table and placed his mobile phone in front of him. He looked over to the counter at the back of the café at the cakes and muffins on display and the Italian biscuits in jars. He turned back to the glass windows and wondered if he had the guts to tell her today. He wanted to. By Christ he wanted to. He straightened up, his elbows on the table, his hands clasped together in front of his face. There'd been some good times, that's for sure. But what the heck. A man's got to do what a man's got to do.

The sliding glass door clanked open and Anny walked in. He looked over at her, first from the rear as she closed the door and then as she approached, her face flushed, her dark hair flying back from her shoulders. Not bad-looking. A bit on the heavy side but not a bad-looker all the same. Yes, there'd been some good times. Especially in the sack.

Anny removed her sunglasses as she walked over and he looked into the bright green of her eyes as she bent down and kissed him on the cheek. He felt the moisture on her face as her skin touched his.

She took off her sunshade and hung it on the back of the chair and sat down. You'll never guess what happened, she said.

What?

I'm still so angry I can hardly speak. She pushed her hair away from her forehead as she dabbed at the sweat with a serviette.

What happened?

This man, she said. This dreadful man. Anny used her fingers to wipe the moisture from under her eyes. I was walking along the cliff path from Bondi to Bronte, like I usually do, minding my own business, when I heard a jogger behind me.

Nothing unusual about that.

So I moved further to the left to let him pass.

Yeah. That's the rules, keep to the left.

He must have been about to pass on the inside because next moment I heard a thud and there he was picking himself up from the side of the track. Anny stopped talking as the waitress approached with notepad and pen.

A spaghetti marinara for me, said Daniel smiling at the waitress. And a coffee.

How do you like your coffee?

He grinned at her. Hot and black, thanks.

Anny turned away from him and squinted at the blackboard. I'll have the Greek salad and a decaf skimmed cap. And a glass of water, please.

And I'll have an orange juice as well, said Daniel.

Daniel's eyes followed the waitress as she walked towards the kitchen. Then his mobile buzzed from the table. He picked it up and held it to his ear.

Yep, he said. I can give them a ballpark figure, but that's about it. Just a ballpark. Yeah, okay then. Here's his number. Daniel opened the front of the phone and pressed a button. 0413 501 583, he said. He put the phone back on the table, its antennae sticking out towards Anny. I hate it when people say things like that, he said.

What?

Oh, nothing. Just the usual crap. They all think they can get something for nothing.

Daniel's pasta arrived first and he began to eat. He sucked in a spaghetti tail and then impatiently cut some of the pasta with his knife. He dispensed with the knife and continued to eat with his fork. He scooped up the marinara with its splayed prongs.

So what happened? he said as he sucked in a loose strand of spaghetti, catching its long skinny tail with his fork.

He must have caught his foot on the edge between the footpath and the grass. I was about to say, 'Are you all right?' when he roared out at me, 'It's all your fault, you know.' 'I was keeping to the left,' I said. He ignored me and ran on, red shiny shorts flapping. How dare he speak to me like that. 'Arsehole,' I called out after him. He gave me the finger up sign and kept running. I was furious.

Daniel didn't answer as he waited for the waitress to place a plate of salad in front of Anny. He blew on his pasta before placing another mouthful towards the back of his tongue, his thin lips closing over the fork.

When I reached Bronte, said Anny, this man had finished his circuit and was on his way back. We recognised each other and he started telling me off about which side of the path I could walk on. 'Don't tell me where to walk, mate,' I hissed. That's when he stopped jogging and moved towards me. I thought he was going to punch me.

Really?

I was a bit scared, I can tell you, but I braced myself. That's when he said, 'You've got some chip on your shoulder because you're fat and ugly.' I laughed at him because it sounded so ridiculous and as far as that was concerned it proved my point. What an arsehole. Just thinking about it makes me angry. .

Daniel turned away from her. He couldn't tell her now. Not after that. He looked out the window to the truck parked across the road. 'Dean's Premium Natural Fruit Juice: the way it should be' emblazoned on the side. The way it should be. That's a bit of a joke. Well, I know this is the way it shouldn't be. He couldn't get Louise out of his head. That last time, her tight white T-shirt over those tight little breasts, leaning over her plate. Eating that huge roll. The sight of her opening her mouth so wide he thought the sides of her lips would crack. Stuffing it in she was. Later at her place when he couldn't wait. Coming up behind her as she cleaned her teeth. Ramming it in.

He tore the crusty white Italian bread into small pieces and used it to mop up the remains of the juice and wiped the red sauce from the corner of his mouth. He reached for his glass and sucked up the remains of his orange juice through a yellowed straw, then burped. He put the glass down, his broad hand wrapped around the grooved surface and leaned across the table.

He looked into Anny's face. I have to go.

Go where?

I'll pay the bill.

What's wrong?

I want to make a move on that Elizabeth Bay deal. He stood up, his keys dangling from the loop at the back of his trousers, his rubber-soled shoes silent as he headed towards the door. Only the sound of his keys and then the bang of the door.

Outside, he pulled out his mobile and dialled. I'm leaving now, honey, he said. I'll be there in a few minutes.

In the café, Anny watched from the window. She sighed, stood up slowly and then walked over to the cake counter. He's a workaholic, that bloke.

I'll have a slice of that chocolate mud cake and a cappuccino, she said to the girl behind the register.

Around the World In Fifty Steps

1. Joanna lives in a Sydney suburb with her two sons. It's 1992 and Australia is in recession.

2. 'I'm sick of licking arse in a service industry,' she says of her marketing business. 'And I'm fed up with financial insecurity, the feast or famine of too many projects or not enough and chasing new business and getting clients to pay their bills.'

3. 'I'm thinking of renting the house out and travelling,' she tells her grown up sons after reading 'The Pitter Patter of Thirty-Year-Old Feet' in the *Sydney Morning Herald*.

4. 'You're ready to leave home are you, Mum?' said one son.

5. 'Why don't you just go on a long holiday instead?' said the other.

6. 'I want a new beginning, a change of career, a new home, a community of people, an intimate relationship with a significant other, that sort of thing.'

7. 'You could always get yourself a dog,' suggests a friend.

8. Her son moves out when she puts his rent up.

9. 'Are you going to wait till he buys a new house for cash before you ask for a decent rent?' her mother had said.

10. 'I've decided to go and live with Dad for a change,' says the other son.

11. 'I'll be away for six to twelve months,' Joanna says as she throws her client files on the rubbish tip.

12. She spends the spring in Italy. The summer in England, Scotland and Ireland. The autumn walking the gorge country of the Ardeche in France.

13. In the winter, she rents a studio apartment in Villefranche on the French Riviera. The studio belongs to a friend of a friend so she's able to get it at a good price. She works as a casual deck hand on one of the luxury cruisers in dry dock for maintenance. 'The first thing I want you to do,' says her boss when she arrives at work on the first day, 'is blitz the tender.' After a backbreaking morning of hard physical work cleaning the small runabout, she goes to lunch. She orders a salad niçoise and a coffee and realises her lunch will cost her a morning's pay.

14. A young and handsome French man who lives in Paris but comes to Villefranche to visit his grandmother most weekends, pursues her. Joanna comes to realise that French men love and cherish women as much as they appreciate good food.

15. She shops at the markets, paints and reads and falls in love with the light and the colours of the south of France.

16. 'I'm able to live contentedly alone without a regular job, without a car, without speaking the language,' she writes to her friends back home.

17. In the summer, she moves on again before the tourist masses arrive and the rent goes up.

18. She gives away to her new friends in Villefranche all the things that won't now fit in her backpack but keeps her paintbrushes and pallet knife.

19. On the Greek island of Skyros she joins a group of landscape artists led by a famous English painter.

20. 'My purpose in leading this group is to help everyone find their own unique style,' says the woman.

21. Joanna spends the autumn in London meeting with other artists from the island, and the woman becomes her mentor and they meet for a cup of tea every week and talk about the isolation of being an artist as well as many other things.

22. 'It's important to stop and regenerate before the creative battery runs flat,' she says.

23. Joanna paints every day and goes out with an Englishman named Clive.

24. 'Your painting is vivid and alive,' says the famous English artist. 'I'll write you a letter of introduction to my contacts in Australia when you're ready to exhibit this collection.'

25. Clive has a strong face with chiselled square cheekbones. Dark brown eyes and dark hair that falls in a square fringe on his forehead. His fingers are long and sensitive for playing the piano.

26. 'What are you doing there?' her mother asks on the phone from across the ocean.

27. 'I'm painting,' says Joanna.

28. 'But what are you doing?'

29. 'My mother is like a poisonous gas that can cross from one side of the world to the other,' Joanna says.

30. Joanna dreams about her sons every night and Clive tells her she cries in her sleep.

31. She yearns for the bright Australian light and for the sound of the ocean.

32. She returns to Australia for her eldest son's wedding.

32. In Sydney, Joanna supplements her income from the house rental by getting a job as a casual for a clothing company. She unpacks boxes and steam presses the garments. Her back, neck and shoulders ache and she suspects she's getting RSI from the steam presser.

33. Clive rings to say he's coming to visit her.

34. In preparation for his arrival she moves all her furniture out of storage and rents a small place near the beach hoping that he'll love it in Australia and decide to stay.

35. Two weeks before his arrival Clive rings to say he's not coming and Joanna finds out through a friend that he's met someone else and is moving in with her.

36. She tears up his photos and throws his Christmas present at the wall.

37. Joanna stops painting.

38. She reflects on the past and all that she's lost.

39. 'I thought when love for you died, I should die. It's dead. Alone, most strangely, I live on.' Rupert Brooke.

40. Joanna stays in bed most days but still feels so tired that she can only remain vertical for four hours in any twenty-four hour period.

41. The phone stops ringing.

42. She rehearses her own death by going to the edge of the cliff.

43. From the edge, she sketches the waves breaking on rocks, the lone seagull on the shore at the water's edge.

44. At home, she fills in the drawing, blending black charcoal and white pastel, reminding herself the darkest hour is before the dawn.

45. And after winter, spring always comes.

46. Joanna sells the house where she lived with her children and spends half the money on a home unit overlooking the ocean and the rest of the money on Australian shares.

47. Her new home faces the east and she can smell the salt from the ocean.

48. 'It takes twenty years to be a successful artist,' echoes in her mind.

50. On a new canvas, she drags the colours of the sunrise across the blank white space.

The New Baby

'Being a parent is harder than being a prime minister,' said British prime minister Tony Blair. His sixteen-year-old son had just been arrested after being found lying drunk on the footpath in London's West End.

In the second month after the baby was born, Kate came out to meet her mother, wiping her hands on her grey tracksuit pants. Kate's hair was tied back off her face revealing tiny white milk spots above her cheeks. Anny told her that already she looked so slim and good. Kate ran her hand over her rounded stomach, arched her back and stuck her belly out at her mother.

They both laughed.

Anny had rushed out early that morning to get to the supermarket before going over to her daughter's house to babysit. But she was happy to be available to help Kate. After all, her own mother had been too busy to help her when Kate was born.

Kate had rung over the weekend and asked what Anny's plans were for Monday.

'I can fit in with you,' her mother had said. 'I can come over whenever it suits you.'

'I'll go to aqua aerobics, then. I should be back by ten-thirty. So if you can get here at nine. And bring lunch.'

'Will I stay on and make dinner?'

'No. Don't stay on.'

'We'll see, then. We'll see how we go.'

After Anny had been to the supermarket, she'd discovered that she'd forgotten to bring the Marie Claire cookbook and the soy sauce, the ginger and the vegetable stock cubes that she had already in her kitchen. So she had to quickly dash back home to Bondi. And then, just before the Cahill Expressway there'd been a breakdown and the traffic was lined up and she was stuck in a bloody traffic jam before reaching the Harbour Tunnel.

'What kept you?' Kate asked by way of a greeting as her mother lifted the shopping bags and the laptop computer out of the boot.

Anny's own body shape was disguised in black trousers and a black V-necked T-shirt, although she'd contrasted and softened the black with a long amethyst necklace.

Kate inspected the necklace around her mother's neck. She picked it up, tugged at it. Banged it playfully against her chest. Is it new? Had she bought it recently? she accused Anny. Or did Anny only imagine it was an accusation? No, it wasn't new. She'd bought the necklace at the markets in Beijing last year when she'd done that cycling in China trip. She'd chosen the stones and had it made up on the spot.

Kate gave her a final inspection. Flicked her eyes up and down her mother's body before giving her the okay to proceed towards the front door.

The windows of the red-brick house rattled as a news helicopter vibrated in towards landing at Gore Hill.

*

Kate and Anny carried the shopping bags to the kitchen. They tiptoed along the wooden corridor past the closed door of the baby's room.

'Don't use the doorbell any more because the noise wakes the baby,' said Kate. 'Just let yourself in with your key.'

Anny breathed in the familiar smell of baby shampoo and fresh linen in the bathroom. The morning sun shone through the blues and reds of the leadlight window, highlighting the plastic baby bath that was turned upside down inside the big bath.

*

Just weeks before the baby was born, Kate and Anny had gone to choose a baby bath. They had already begun the habit of Mondays together. It had taken ages to find the right white plastic baby bath. They must have looked at every bath in Chatswood. Kate had wanted one that had a hole down one end and a plug so she could empty the bath without tipping the whole thing up. They'd walked the length and breadth of Chatswood.

Back home, they'd rearranged things in the spare room to make space for the baby. They'd emptied drawers, taken underwear and socks out of one place and stacked them in with others, reorganised the shelves of the laundry, relocated Kate's husband's wine collection.

Dan didn't complain about his wine being relocated, but he did say he didn't want his mother-in-law handling his underwear. 'It's all a matter of intimacy and certain things being private,' he'd said.

In the weeks after the baby was born, Anny had come over every day to help. She'd cleaned up the kitchen, unstacked the dishwasher, made lunch, folded up the clean linen, brought the washing in.

*

As Anny unpacked the shopping, Kate gave her mother the instructions. 'Don't feed him before ten. Preferably not before ten-thirty. The breast milk is in a bottle in the fridge.'

'Yes. I didn't realise that it's better to feed him later rather than sooner so he's more willing to take the bottle from me.'

Last time, Kate had come home early and he'd refused the bottle because he could smell his mother and knew he had a better option.

'Run the water from cold to hot,' Kate continued. 'Then let it sit in the hot water for five minutes. Check it on the inside of your wrist. And don't forget to give it a good shake.'

'Yes. Yes. I know how to do it but show me again anyway.'

In the small bright kitchen, two hand-painted ceramic plates were secured on either side of the wooden window that looked out on to the backyard. Anny put the food into the fridge and then set up the computer on the dining room table.

Kate waited by the front door for her friend.

She sat down on the steps.

*

The wind picked up, flapping the blue and white awning of the house next door. In the front garden, a pile of magnolia petals lay in a heap on the grass. Kate sat there at the top of the stone steps at the front door. She leant down. Rested her head in her hands. She felt the pounding of her heart against her chest, the cold sweat on her hands. She tried to breathe in. Tried to slow her breathing. She'd never had this before. Gasping for breath. It would happen even when she was lying on her bed trying to rest. Her heart would bang hard against her. Bang, bang, bang. Expecting the baby to wake at any moment. The sensation frightened her. Was she going crazy? And the recurring nightmares. The house burning down and she couldn't get the baby out in time. And the crying, wanting to cry all the time. And at strange times. Like when she was out shopping with the baby. She couldn't even go shopping and get a couple of things without him putting on a performance.

*

Anny heard her in the hallway pacing up and down. 'Why don't you ring and check your friend is coming for sure?' she said to her daughter.

'Because we spoke only yesterday and confirmed the arrangement.' Kate couldn't keep the irritation out of her voice. She walked down the hallway and into the bedroom to check the time on the clock beside the bed. She sat down on the white linen bedspread. Looked across at the antique pine dressing table and her books piled high: *Settling Techniques*; *Newborn to 6 Months*; *The Baby 0–9 Months*; *Motherhood: making it work for you*; *Meditations for Women Who Do Too Much*; *The Baby Swings Book*; *Baby Love*.

She got up and went back into the kitchen to look at the time on the microwave clock. 'Damn it,' said Kate. 'Now we'll be late for the class.'

'Why don't you go on your own and I'll tell her that you've gone when she arrives?'

A car door slammed outside.

Kate picked up her swimming bag and hurried to the door. It was someone for next door. She came back in.

Anny suggested again that she ring her friend and say she'd meet her there.

Kate checked the time on my watch. Then picked up the cordless phone and dialled. 'I thought I could meet you there,' she said into the phone. 'I thought you might be rushing and it would save you some time.'

Silence as she listened to her friend's reply.

'Tell her you'll meet her there,' Anny insisted.

'I'll wait then,' Kate sighed into the phone. She hung up. With the phone still in her hand, she moved towards her mother. Her eyebrows were pressed together in an angry frown. She used the aerial of the phone to prod Anny in the arm. 'Stop it,' she hissed. 'Just stop it.'

*

'Stay out as long as you like,' Anny encouraged when Kate's friend finally pulled up in the car. 'Make the most of it. If I need you, I can ring on the mobile.'

Kate hoisted her swimming bag up on to her shoulder. Kissed her mother on the cheek.

'I can handle him,' Anny assured her. 'I feel confident. The only thing I can't manage is if he gets hysterical like he did last night.'

'Take him for a walk in the pram if he cries too much. He got hysterical last night because he was overtired.'

Anny waved goodbye from the front door.

*

After Kate left, Anny swung into action. Watered the pot plants, adjusted her rearrangements from last week – moved the wooden plant stand from the lounge room to the dining room, the blue and white porcelain plant holder to the top of the plant stand. Kate said it was okay. If Dan didn't like the rearranging, he'd put everything back where it was.

Eleven-fifteen and no sound yet from the baby's room. Anny shut down the computer and went into his room to check he was still breathing. She opened his door moving quietly as she stepped over a teddy bear on the floor. She approached his white-painted cradle and looked down at him as he lay on his back, his head slightly to the side and tipped down against his chest. His long eyelashes fluttered against his cheeks, the tip of his button nose catching the light from the window. His rosebud lips pulsed ever so slightly together.

When he woke up, she warmed the milk and carried him into the lounge room. She held him close against her body for the twenty minutes it took him to drink the bottle. One of his tiny perfect hands stayed wrapped around her thumb.

*

The drought in NSW continued through the winter. 'Even Sydney has experienced one of the driest stretches since European settlement,' said Agriculture Minister Richard Amery.

Anny had been to the gym and hoped to ease the aches in her legs by relaxing in a hot bath. The telephone rang while she was running the bath. She stopped and listened and then switched off the taps. She went to answer the telephone. 'Hello,' she said. 'Anny here.'

147

'Mum, it's me.'

'How are you, darling? I've been thinking about you and wondering how you were going.'

'I so much didn't want this to happen,' she said. 'I was at breaking point. Things were getting worse and worse. But they've looked after me here. They've looked after me very well.'

'That's good, darling,' Anny said, trying to sound calm and positive.

'I expressed for the last couple of days and they gave him the bottle at three-thirty in the morning. He slept for seven hours last night. The first time ever. And the first time I've slept deeply since he was born.'

Anny could hear gentle classical music playing in the background.

'Who wouldn't go a bit mad with the sleep deprivation alone?' said Kate. 'Let alone all the other stuff. And the hormone thing. It's like having PMT for three months.'

'So what do you think you've learnt from the week?'

'I suppose for me not to feel that I have to be totally responsible and committed to him twenty-four hours a day, and being with mothers in a similar situation helps too. That there are a lot of people whose support I can utilise. I was able to hand over to the midwives and have a rest. It took the whole responsibility off me. They pretty much said that he'd picked up where I was at.'

'Did they say anything else?'

'Take a chill pill.'

'A chill pill? How will you do that?'

'It's an expression. Try and go with the flow much more. They said it's not good for the baby for me to be like this, which makes me feel great! They offered to show me more information about the effects on the baby, but I didn't want to see. My counsellor said that people like me are much more connected. We are sensitive and intelligent people. Qualities that she really likes in a person. I asked her couldn't I just do cognitive behaviour therapy, and go to yoga twice a week. She said all those things will help, but they won't change the brain chemistry. And she said I'll bash myself up even more because I'm not able to change my thinking with the CBT.'

From the window, as Anny watched, a storm came in, rolling in across the dark metallic grey of the sea. She cradled the phone between her neck and her shoulder. Pressed her hands against the window. Felt the cold glass against her palms. Watched the imprint of hands recede as she held the phone to her ear.

'So what can the people who love and care about you do for you?' she said.

'When someone is at my place that I can go out and have a break from him. Giving me time away from him. I was thinking of going home for a week or two and see how I feel before making a decision about going on medication.'

The first of the rain started to fall as Anny watched.

'I always felt total love and connection to him,' said Kate. 'But I knew he was unhappy and there was nothing I could do. That was very painful for me. To see my baby so distressed and not being able to do anything for him.'

The wind blew the leaves on the trees in front of Anny helter skelter as the storm built up. Hail the size of small marbles landed on the railing of the balcony, bounced to the ground, hit the pot plants.

'I may go into denial when I get home,' said Kate. 'I need you and Dan to tell me if I get worse. I need Dan to say, "Honey, you're getting worse." You could say that to me too. So how's the week been for you?'

'Okay. I didn't worry too much about you because I knew you were in good hands – that you were being looked after. I knew you were in the best possible place. I didn't worry as much as I do sometimes. It's hard not to because we're so inter…interconnected. You and me.'

'Interwoven.'

'Yes. That's a better word. Interwoven. We're interwoven.'

The rain eased. The pot plants all wet and shiny.

'How did the parents' night go at the hospital?'

'The idea was for the fathers to talk about how they're feeling but it

didn't turn out that way. They got on to talking about settling the baby
– and the conversation stayed on settling.'

*

Anny walked into the bathroom and turned the taps back on. She
added a scoop of Radox, picked up a washer from the end of the bath.
She warmed it in the hot water, pressed it against her face. Then lay
back against the porcelain. She closed her eyes. Thought about her own
feeling of helplessness as she'd watched her daughter in distress.

She remembered when Kate was a baby. Her own mother's
nagging. Was the baby getting enough to eat? Did Anny have enough
breast milk? The constant worrying about why the baby was crying.
And her mother undermining her confidence, telling her that the baby
was crying because she didn't have enough milk to feed her baby.

'Shut the door and walk away,' was her mother's advice. But the
doctor had said she wasn't to leave Kate to cry. He said Kate was a
sensitive baby and would withdraw from her if she was left alone to cry.

Anny rubbed the coarse fabric up and down her arms, then up and
down her legs. She lay in the bath for a time and then got out. She looked
in the mirror as she dried herself. Turned her body sideways to the mirror.
Pulled her stomach in, tucked her bottom under, stood up straight.

*

A warm day. Anny watched the sun rise in the morning. Saw the red
sun hidden behind a cluster of clouds. The colours of the clouds
changed each part of a second as she watched. More pink. Less mauve.
The glow extended out along the horizon. The sea flat. The birds
making noises like soft percussion triangles.

*

Kate and her mother sat on the floor of the bathroom as Kate bathed the baby in the big bath. A deep old-fashioned porcelain bath perched above black and white tiles. Kate kept splashing warm water on to his back to keep him warm as he stood up inspecting the taps, investigating the exit of the water from the faucet. His back wet and shiny. His bottom dimpled.

Kate looked across at her mother, a frown on her face and a dipped inflection in her voice. 'I heard a terrible story this week, she said. 'It's a horrible story.'

Anny could tell by Kate's tone that perhaps it would be better if she didn't tell her the story. But she didn't say so. She took a deep breath instead.

'You know Vivian who lives across the road?' Kate said. 'Vivian from the mothers' group.'

Anny nodded.

'Well, it's a friend of Vivian's. They've known each other since they were children, and their mothers are friends. The friend's mother thought her daughter seemed not herself after the birth of the baby. The friend's mother had said to her son-in-law that she wanted to discuss it with him. Before she was able to talk to him, the daughter tried to kill her husband. She attacked him. Tried to strangle him. Then she jumped off the balcony with the baby in her arms.'

'Oh no! That's dreadful!'

'The baby died and the woman is in hospital.'

'That's a dreadful, dreadful story.'

'She'd thought that if she killed the whole family, then they'd all be together in heaven.'

The baby sat down in the bath, then picked up a blue plastic scooper and used it to drink the bathwater. He smiled up at Kate and Anny as they leant over the bath. He pushed some plastic toys down from the side of the bath and watched the toys splash into the water.

'How will it be for her when she realises she's killed her baby?' said Kate. 'And what about her relationship with her husband?'

Anny and Kate looked at each other. Kate reached down and

picked the baby up out of the bath. As she wrapped a towel around him, he put his arms down by his sides and leant his head against her chest. She held him tight against her.

*

Anny could hear Kate and her friend and the friend's baby as they came in the front door. Kate introduced the friend to her mother. Her name was Alice. Anny offered Alice a cup of tea and the three of them sat around the dining room table. They drank tea out of pretty china cups – half open buds and violets and forget-me-nots. The midday sun slanted through the window.

Alice fidgeted with the teaspoon on her saucer. She picked the spoon up, turned it over, put it down again. 'I wish my mother was here,' she said.

'Where's your mother?' Anny asked.

'In England. She lives in England. England is so far away. I ring her up but she's busy doing her thing. And my father complains about the phone bills.'

'That's a shame,' Anny commiserated.

Alice's baby watched her, listened, turned his head towards her. Her voice lowered. 'It would be so nice to sit down with my mother and to be able to talk like this. To be able to say, "The baby did this or she did that. The baby rolled over."'

Kate and Anny looked at each other and nodded in agreement.

*

Anny remembered the last time she had seen her own mother. Anny had always felt that her mother wasn't any good at the business of mothering. Motherhood hadn't come easily to her. Perhaps she should never have been a mother; certainly she was one too soon. But hers was not an age in which women felt they had a choice.

It was five years ago now since that afternoon before she died. They were sitting in the visitors' sunroom of the Jewish Hospital in Woollahra. Her mother's hair an immaculate coiffure as always. A pale pink dressing gown tied around her waist. Anny had rung her children and arranged to meet them at the hospital. What she remembers most clearly about that afternoon is her mother's anger because Anny had taken so long to wash and dry one of her nighties. Taken longer than her older sister, who usually took the dirty nighties home and who had a clothes dryer. Anny had hung the nightie on a clothesline in the sun in her backyard and she'd thought it smelt particularly fresh and clean. But her mother was angry with her for not bringing the nightie back sooner. What took her so long? Wasn't there anything she could do properly? Couldn't she get anything right?

*

The scent of spring jasmine in the cooling air. A row of cherry blossom trees blossomed soft pink against dark wooden stems. Anny stood at the front door and waved goodbye to Alice as Kate helped her out to the car. She looked across at a blood-red hibiscus in the garden next door. A dog asleep on the grass.

Kate came back and stood beside her mother at the front door. Put her arm all the way around her. Patted her on the back. They leant into each other. Then went inside and closed the front door.

Tell Me About What Happened On New Year's Eve

I'd looked out the top-floor hospital window towards Coogee to the night sky lit by fireworks and saw the miserable face of the moon and thought that I'd never felt as detached from life as at that moment. At the same time, I realised that I probably felt so despicable due to the weeks spent lying in hospital and the excruciatingly slow and painful road to recovery. By sheer force of will, I stopped looking at the dark mirror of the moon. No one could have told me how much the distant celebrations, the sound of the explosions and the changing shapes and colours of the fireworks could jolt me into the present and away from the unbearable lethargy, the severed muscles and tendons and the nausea caused by the drugs and painkillers. Was it that I could sense, without glancing up again, that clouds were making their way across the moon and that made me realise: how would it be to feel this would be your last new year?

It's Pot Luck When You Move Into a Unit

A nice quiet weekend? the woman downstairs said.

What do you mean? I said, through the open back door, a bag of rubbish in each hand.

She smoothed her ironing on the board and said, They weren't around over the weekend – with the baby. She looked happy.

I'm lucky living on the top floor, I said.

She nodded towards the other side of the building. Jim isn't so lucky – he's got the woman upstairs, she said. When he plays the piano and she thumps on the floor. She put the iron back on its stand. She's heavy-footed, that woman. Bang, bang, bang. I hear her coming down the stairs every morning at six, and the slam of the front door.

That night, the wind knocked my vase off the window ledge. I lay awake wondering if the noise of the smash had woken up the people underneath – the ones whose barbecuing sends smoke and disgusting meat smells into my unit. Nothing clings to your furniture like the stink from last week's burnt fat. Sorry about the crash, I muttered to the floor, It was the wind.

In Retreat

It's New Year's Eve and I'm driving west from Sydney to a health retreat near Penrith. The retreat is only about an hour and a half out of Sydney but, knowing my appalling navigation skills, I've allowed myself four hours to get there. Driving is not my forte. A car gets me from point A to point B but I do prefer the public transport option when it's available. I suppose I'm one of the only people in Sydney with this particular preference.

New Year's Eve is something I have to plan for each year to avoid, God forbid, spending the holiday break alone. It seems that 'everyone else' is spending New Year with Loved Ones and because I'm not, I feel like a total failure. A social misfit. So I've left my home by the sea at Bondi and come out west.

I'd said to my daughter that I'll probably be in bed with a book by nine o'clock on New Year's Eve.

'You won't, will you?' Kate said with disbelief. 'That's what I'll be doing, not you. That's something I'd say, not you.'

Kate is staying with her husband at his parents' holiday house on the beach down south. Not that I'm expecting to meet anyone on this holiday. But I'm always interested to hear how couples meet – at the bus stop, the petrol station, at work, mutual friends, a common interest? – to hear how two lives become intertwined. How of the nearly infinite number of possible conjunctions this or that one comes into being, to hear the first chapter of a story in progress. I think a lot about endings in my own life, so it's a relief, a sort of holiday, to visit the realm of beginnings.

So far on this drive out west I've only made two wrong turns and had to turn back twice. My hands and arms ache from clutching the steering wheel. My neck and shoulders ache from being hunched over. My neck must be jutting forward in an unnatural position.

After twenty minutes on the expressway, I stop for a breather at the pull-over petrol station. Believe it or not, it's my first time driving on this expressway towards the Blue Mountains. I usually catch a leisurely train if I'm travelling in this direction, but my friend Simon said I should drive to the retreat rather than use a train and a bus because he said I'll need a car to go down the road to the local café for a cappuccino.

The concentration on driving is making me nervous – my stress levels are rising. At this pull-over point, the only mistake I make so far is to drive into the truck entrance instead of the car entry. I eat my banana in the car in between the trucks then buy a bottle of Diet Coke. As I drive out on the truck exit, I reflect that this could be my last good hit of caffeine for a week.

The retreat is a long low bungalow-style building at the end of a residential street with grassy paddocks beyond and in the distance. It takes me a couple of goes to manoeuvre my car into alignment with the other cars in the one remaining covered car space beside the main building.

Some people come to this health retreat to lose weight, others to give up smoking, some to do battle with cancer, some for pure indulgence. I've come for the pure indulgence idea, although I've brought my computer, mainly for emailing purposes.

Health retreats are my preferred kind of holiday. Lots of physical activity, communal meals. You can be with people if you want to or you can be alone. Gourmet vegetarian food, a gym, yoga, meditation, talks on healthy living, aquarobics, cycling. Or maybe I'll just lie around reading all day by the swimming pool – not that that's likely.

I lift my very small suitcase on wheels out of the boot, and the laptop, and head for Reception, very pleased that I'm still able to travel so light, even though I had the whole car to fill up if I'd wanted to. It's good to keep in travel-light training – on the ready for the next big adventure.

A woman of about my age (my unspecified age) greets me at Reception. She leads me along the winding path past the herb garden and the swimming pool to the back of the property to my room. My booking is for a one-week Pamper Package. This allows me to have a massage each day, all inclusive in the price, so I'll be forced to indulge. And I've booked a balcony room with facilities, not my usual holiday booking of a budget room with a share bathroom.

My suitcase wheels slip and slide along the cobbled pathway with a bump and a crunch but the suitcase remains upright as it's light and easy to guide along between the grassy verges. Good to be independent and able to manage the transport of one's own luggage. We pass other guests lounging by the swimming pool, some asleep with books on their laps, some reading in the silent area outside the massage rooms.

I'm able to afford this rather expensive holiday because I've just finished making a ceramic dinner set that some wealthy people commissioned me to make. I'm rather pleased with the dinner set actually. I used images from the circus as a connecting theme, so each plate is different from the other. I didn't have to keep reproducing the same boring design. Every piece is complete but different from the others, linked by the animals and the various circus acts. The problem, though, with doing commissioned work is that you have to keep the client in mind all the time – Will they like it? Is this what they want? – rather than being free to paint whatever you like. I'd much prefer to be working towards an exhibition. Then people either like what you've made and buy it, or they don't. But then the amount of work, money and effort involved in mounting an exhibition is horrendous.

I ask the woman from Reception if the people who come here are mostly from Sydney.

'Oh, yes,' she says. 'In fact, most of them seem to come from Bondi. If not Bondi, then the eastern suburbs at least.'

She unlocks the door to my room and I'm very happy with what I see.

Big sliding glass doors that overlook a valley, trees, grass, a small terracotta-tiled cottage in the distance against a tree-covered hill. The room is decorated in shades of apricot and turquoise. A television set up on the wall, a clock radio, a Van Gogh print, *Femme en Provence*, above the wall heater. Monet's *La Maison du Jardinier* above the king-size bed. A red emergency call button on the wall. On a small round glass coffee table, a tray with two glass jars: peppermint tea bags and chamomile. No fridge in the room that could hold the milk that I'd like to have in a cup of tea that I could make with my tea bags brought from home. In the bathroom a sign: 'Place tampons and sanitary pads in the bin provided. Bins are emptied daily. Toilet, bath and basin are on a septic system.' There's a shower but no bath.

'Is there a bath somewhere on the premises that I can use?' I ask.

'There's one in the main building, next door to the video room,' the woman from Reception says as she goes out the door.

An announcement booms over the loudspeaker: 'Lunch is now being served in the dining room.' Walking towards the dining room, I meet Alexandra, an older frail woman who uses a walking frame that takes up the width of the hallway. To facilitate her journey to the dining room and to unblock the hallway, I help her by opening the glass doors that lead from outside through the lounge room past Reception and along the hallway into the dining room.

The dining room is composed of large round tables for eight. In the middle of each is a jar of Promite, a jar of honey, a pepper grinder. Some tables have Reserved signs on them. One has a sign, 'Silent Table'.

My friend Simon had told me about the Silent Table – for people who find it too tiring and stressful to engage in conversation and answer the endless questions. I will see Simon here next weekend when he comes on Sunday to give a yoga class and a couple of lectures. I'm looking forward to seeing him, as we always have a few laughs. Simon and his partner come here once a month to teach. They also book in to fast a couple of times a year – juices only, for body cleansing. I'm definitely not here to fast. I wouldn't be paying all this money to stay resting in my room drinking juices all day.

Guests are queued up at the long buffet table. The table is spread with salads of leafy dark greens, and in two big hot silver containers are a variety of hot vegetables. Tofu and a small amount of white cheese can be glimpsed under spinach and pumpkin and tomatoes. In tiny bowls with a teaspoon beside them are chopped walnuts, almonds and brazils. At the end of the table, assorted plates of cherries, mangoes, pineapple, peaches, plums, black grapes, green grapes, kiwis and strawberries. I pile up my plate and then join a table with two other women. They introduce themselves.

In the area off the dining room, people on a fast, who choose not to have their juices delivered to their rooms by a trolley, sit separately from the rest of the guests sipping their juices. People on special diets also sit in this area separated from the huge buffet table and the dining room.

Amid the chatter of voices and the clattering of cutlery, a man comes over and sits next to me. He introduces himself. His name is Lachlan. He looks okay. About my age, not fat, not bald. An average sort of a bloke, but a rare species in a place like this. He wears black Buddy Holly-style glasses, shorts, a T-shirt and the obligatory walker's sandals. I'm trying hard to be interested in men my own age. My daughter especially would like me to behave in a manner that is more appropriate to my age.

'Is this your first time here?' Lachlan asks.

'Yes, first time. You?'

'I've been here eight times before.'

'Really?'

At that moment, he pulls a neatly ironed handkerchief from his pocket and sneezes into it. 'I like it here,' he says.

I avert my eyes as he cleans up his nose. 'I hope you're not going to spread your germs,' I say in a jokey voice.

He doesn't respond to my comment but we move on to talk about other health retreats and health and fitness generally and he seems to have a good grasp of what constitutes healthy lifestyle, or I assume this about him. I find an interest in healthy lifestyle to be an attractive quality about a man – an openness to try alternative therapies. Or, to be more precise, someone not rigid, someone open to possibilities by trying new things.

He starts in on his salad, scraping the plate as he eats. 'My aim on this holiday is to get fitter,' he says. 'So I don't spend the whole holiday asleep. I realised I had to get myself into good health when my wife died, or the children would have no one.'

'What happened to your wife?'

'She smoked and drank too much. Had emphysema. Died of pneumonia in the end.'

I want to ask more to find out how a woman who is not very old dies from smoking and drinking too much. But I don't like to probe. 'When did she die?'

'It's six years now.' He sniffs inwards. 'When did you get here?' he says.

'About twenty minutes ago.' I expand on the details of my arrival by telling him that it was a big achievement for me to find my way to this place. 'I've never driven along the expressway before. I don't like driving on the expressway. You can't blow your nose, eat a banana, or do anything else you might feel like,' I add in my joking voice.

He looks at me blankly. 'What do you think of it here?'

'It looks pretty good so far. I've got a fabulous room. A beautiful balcony looking down the valley.'

'I booked in at the last moment, so I missed out on one of those balcony rooms. I'm down the back in a big room – big enough to sleep five people.' He returns to eating his food.

More women join the table and introductions are exchanged.

'It's nice to have a man at the table for a change,' someone says.

Questions are asked and answered. Have you been here before? Why are you here? What sort of package did you book?

One woman says she's brought her own instant coffee, but doesn't like to drink it black and has nowhere to store some milk.

'I'll bring a little esky next time,' I say. 'I've brought my own tea bags in order to avoid the caffeine withdrawal headaches.'

'That's a good idea.'

'Why go through the pain of headaches that ruin your holiday if you plan to drink caffeine again anyway when you go back home?'

One woman says something along the lines of wanting to prove to herself that she can give up caffeine if she wants to, and that if she's here to improve her health she'll not drink it.

A young woman sits down in the last vacant seat. She wears a tracksuit, joggers and holds an eyeshade in her hand. Her glossy blonde hair is pushed back off her high forehead and brushed in a long curve behind her ears, where it curls slightly beneath the groove left by her shade. Her name is Felicity. She runs a ceramic studio at Randwick. She says she loves painting ceramics and now she's teaching it. She's successfully made the change from an office job to a job she really enjoys. I tell her about my kiln in the garage.

'What do you make?' Felicity asks.

'My specialty is watery themes. Mermaids. Mermaids and other fishy things. I've done a few commissioned pieces.'

'Really?'

'A series of border tiles for a shop in Newtown, soap pumps for a gift shop at Double Bay.'

'That's pretty good. I've only sold my work at the markets so far. Mosman and Rozelle. But it's hard to make money and it's a bit of a drag having to set it all up and carry the ceramics from the car and then sit around all day at a card table.'

'Ceramic painting is very labour-intensive,' I hear myself sigh. 'Hard to make money out of it.'

'It's hard,' Felicity agrees.

We continue eating.

'Have you been here before?' I ask Felicity.

'Twice before and both times I was on a fast. Recovering from glandular fever.'

'What was it like, being on a fast?'

'After the first couple of days, you don't crave food. You don't have that empty feeling. Your body goes into starvation mode and feeds off itself. But every time you look at the television or open a magazine, you see an ad for food and that makes you think of how much you enjoy eating. The fast is an inward journey. You stay in your room a lot because that's all you feel like doing. You sleep a lot. Maybe join a class or go to a talk. Read. I wrote in my diary because you focus in on yourself. I felt like writing.'

I nod with understanding before the two of us get up to return to the buffet table for seconds.

'You need to get the fruit early,' Felicity advises. 'Before all the good pieces are taken. The mangoes and cherries go very quickly. It's best to get a plate of fruit with your main course so you don't miss out.'

Back at the table, Lachlan initiates further conversation. 'What sort of work do you do?' he asks me.

'A bit of this and that,' I say grinding black pepper on to the salad.

'You keep yourself out of mischief?'

If there's one thing I can't stand, it's that expression, 'keep yourself out of mischief'. So I explain to Lachlan that I prefer not to say what I do, especially when I'm on holidays. I like to come to a place like this and not talk about work.

'Maybe at the end of the week we can tell each other what we do,' I say in an effort to appear friendly still.

He shrugs.

'I used to tell people as a joke that I'm retired from the circus,' I add. 'The first time I said it, I expected the person to realise I was joking. It was some personal growth course I was on and we'd been told to experiment. To say we were a lion tamer or something and see what reactions we'd get. So when I said tightrope walker, I expected the person who asked the question to know I'd made it up. But she was very interested to know about life in the circus and word soon spread and people kept coming up to me during the holiday and asking me questions about my life in the circus.'

'Such as?'

'Were my parents in the circus? Had I met my husband in the circus? Where did I train? What sort of rope was the tightrope? I told them it was a hard life being in the circus. Living out of a suitcase, constantly having to move on. A lot of hours. Only one day off a week. Circus life was tough, very tough. I said that it wears on you mentally and physically. And that performing in a circus is hard on your body. Trapeze had always been my first love, I said, and my father was a PE teacher. But now I'm sick of saying I used to work in the circus. People keep asking me the same boring questions about my life as a tightrope walker.'

'I could imagine you in a sequinned costume up on the tightrope,' says Felicity.

'The problem was that I said I was a tightrope walker. What I meant to say was, trapeze artiste. My real fantasy was to be able to feel free as a bird, to be able to fly through the air like a trapeze artiste. Because the true story is that what I am in my life is a tightrope walker.'

No one comments. The fans whir against the ceiling.

'Is it still hot outside?' I ask Felicity.

'Very hot. Yes, and I think it will be hot into the night. The reception area is air conditioned. They plan to put air conditioning in the whole place. With the next big bequest.'

I stand up, excuse myself and head for the area in the hallway outside the dining room where the day's activities are set out on a large board against the wall. I could join in the afternoon's cycle but it really is too hot outside to be going anywhere. A nice relax in the bath would be better. And anyway, the organised cycle is unlikely to be a good workout. I'll only get irritated going at a snail's pace.

Lachlan calls out after me. 'See you later, then.'

He could be interesting. Although he was very evasive about his wife's death, which was puzzling. He'd said his wife only wanted to live at the end. But by then it was too late.

On the way to find the bath in my skimpy dress with a towel over one shoulder and nothing on underneath and in a hurry to secure a vacant bathroom and averting my eyes because I have no make-up on and without my contact lenses, Lachlan comes walking along the corridor towards me. From a distance, and with blurred vision, the figure coming towards me looks like a woman. A handsome woman, but then I hadn't expected to see him.

'My daughter likes to take a bath,' he says. ' Have you booked in to have an aromatherapy bath?'

'No, I've brought some of my own oils to put in the bath.'

'I've brought some eucalyptus oil but I'd like to buy some others.'

I was about to ask him some question on this point, but he broke off suddenly to gaze down towards the video room.

'There's a Diet for All Reasons video about to start,' he says. 'I'll see you later.'

It's New Year's Eve evening. Lachlan and I are walking around the block. At dinner he'd suggested we go on a walk after he's finished playing Pictionary. Surprisingly, the retreat had nothing planned for this evening. It seems as if all the staff have gone home and the guests are left to entertain themselves. Sitting at dinner with the others it felt like any other old night of the week rather than New Year's Eve, when someone had suggested we play a game of Pictionary. I'd declined the invitation but said that I'd watch. I mean, it wasn't even dark yet. Far too early to be going back to my room and to bed. But before we'd gone into the lounge to find the Pictionary, we'd eaten the fruit cake left over from Christmas Day and the extra cherries that the kitchen staff left out as a special treat.

'I like the night sounds,' says Lachlan as we walk past the red-brick suburban houses towards the town.

We pass three teenage boys burrowing under the bonnet of a Holden.

'What night sounds do you like?' he asks.

Without realising that I'm not really answering his question, I tell him the night sounds that I find scary at home are the wind whistling up the gully near my home, water pouring down from the waterfall, the crashing of the ocean against rocks at night.

'Those are sounds you don't like,' he points out in an irritated voice. 'What sounds do you like?'

Because I can't think of any night sounds that I do like, I don't say anything. I'm afraid of the night – but I don't tell him that. Why would I want to be telling him about my fear of the dark, the recurring nightmares that plague me?

Changing the subject I ask, 'What did you do on Christmas Day?'

'I spent the whole day asleep. The best gift I could give myself.'

As we walk, I find it difficult to see because now we've left the street lights and are heading out towards the fields.

Trying to sound positive and as if I'm enjoying walking in the dark even when I can't see a bloody thing, I say, 'I can smell blossoms, wet grass and hay.'

'There are rabbits in the bush. Down in the valley near the Nepean River.'

'I'd prefer to walk where it's well lit.'

'I'm training myself to see without my glasses. It's good to train yourself to be able to see where there's not much light.' He goes on to say he's done some course or other to learn how to see without glasses and now he'd like to teach the method to other people.

I concentrate on not twisting my ankle on any of the potholes in the road that I can't see. We walk along the road towards any oncoming traffic that may appear.

He says that his birthmark has helped him to be accepting of people with a handicap. I hadn't noticed his birthmark but now I glance at his bare legs but I can't see anything.

'Where did you grow up?' I ask.

'In Canberra, with my two brothers and two sisters. I'm the only one who got out. I used to represent Canberra in football.' He sniffs inwards with a loud snuffling sound. 'Do you play tennis?'

'Yes I do. But I haven't been playing much because of tennis elbow.'

'They've got a court at the retreat. We could have a game.'

'Are you any good?'

'We used to play once a week. We'd get a babysitter.'

Oh yes, I think, as if he'd be any good playing only once a week, and mixed doubles at that. I don't say to him that I only play tennis with people who can play well. Nothing worse than trying to hit soft piddly balls.

We retrace our steps to the retreat. Everyone seems to have gone to bed, so we sit in the foyer near Reception and have a cup of tea. There is a trolley outside the dining room with pots of fresh ginger in large silver tea pots and a jar of honey with a wooden spiral ladle. Lachlan pours the tea for the two of us, adds the honey and stirs both cups. I like it when a man serves me food or drink with concentrated effort and care. Then we go into the gym, where there's a small TV set up on the wall to watch the end of the New Year fireworks. We sit in the middle of the gymnasium on white plastic chairs from Reception and watch the final minutes of the spectacular display of colour and light taking place on Sydney Harbour.

It's New Year's Day. Opening the heavy curtains to a clear, light grey-blue sky, I hear the tinkling sounds of bellbirds and the occasional moo. The cows were frantic earlier in the morning. They must have needed milking. On the radio, a man says it will be mostly fine and very very pleasant. And that in Beijing the thud of a giant bell welcomed the New Year, in Japan bells rang a hundred and eight times to ring out the bad spirits, in China there was a mass wedding for five hundred couples at the Great Wall.

I pick up the telephone and ring my children. I wish them a happy new year. My daughter asks if there's anyone nice here. I tell her about Felicity and about going for a walk with Lachlan.

At breakfast, the buffet is laden with fruit cut into wedges. At the tables that have guests' names displayed, diced pawpaw fill the white bowls beside each name.

'Pawpaw is very good for digestion,' says Felicity, 'but needs to be eaten on its own.'

'Interesting,' I say. 'I must eat it more often at home. Did you sleep well?'

'Reasonably well. I got up in the middle of the night and turned the fan off.'

'I must say I was desperate for breakfast. It seems to be a long wait from waking until breakfast time.'

'You can help yourself to fruit from the fruit bowl.'

'I know. But I still felt ravenous. What was the seaweed wrap like yesterday?'

'Good. You get wrapped in plastic and a blanket, then shower. She left my spare undies in a plastic bag in the seat in the shower room then did a fabulous massage. She used some reiki healing as well. Said my neck was very tight.' Felicity gets up to return to the buffet and then comes back to the table with rice-cake biscuits covered in tahini.

'This diced fresh fruit is wonderful,' says a woman across the table. 'I don't bother to cut fruit up for myself at breakfast time. Only for my children's breakfasts.'

'You should think of yourself as another child,' suggests a grey-haired man at the table. 'And cut some fruit up for yourself.'

This man's name is Ray. He's widowed and very sought-after by the older women here, who hurry to sit next to him and to entertain him with any fascinating stories they can think up.

'I'm tempted to try food combining,' says Felicity.

'But it's so hard not to have rice with your stirfry.'

'I've decided to try food combining for my wind problem,' says Ray. 'To keep proteins and carbohydrates separate at each meal because I seem to have a big digestive problem at the moment. What do you think about food combining?' he asks me.

'You need both protein and carbohydrate in a meal or else you have no energy.'

'The food here doesn't leave me satisfied. My stomach rumbles all the time.'

'But it is yummy. I might have to buy the recipe book.'

'Another idea is that carbohydrates turn to sugar and it's better to be eating lots of protein. Less bread, pasta and potatoes.'

We continue eating, spoons scraping against bowls.

Felicity leans towards me and speaks in a lowered voice. 'My boyfriend is coming to visit for the day tomorrow. I'm going to ask him to give me a massage.'

'A massage by a partner is not as good as the real thing,' interrupts the young married woman with small children sitting next to us. 'My husband could give me a massage but he's just not as good as the real thing.'

'Some of them are,' disagrees Felicity with a rising inflection in her voice.

'No,' says the woman. 'They think they are, though.'

'Some of us are,' says Lachlan with a smug grin.

A pale light filters through a large window in front of Reception. The guests are gathered there for the five o'clock soup that is available on one of the large silver trolleys. Dinner time is an hour away. The woman who is staying in the room next to mine is telling me that she also lives in Bondi, that she works as a lawyer, is single and has brought her own caffeine hit: a tin of instant coffee. This woman is attractive with full lips, open round face, shoulder-length dark hair. The skin on her face is smooth and has a healthy glow.

'Next time, I'll book for a five-day stay rather than seven,' she says. 'I feel caged in and I'm missing my friends.'

'You can ring them up.'

'It's expensive from here, isn't it?'

'I don't care. I've made a couple of calls.'

'My awning has become stuck. And now I can't get it to go up and so I feel boxed in now that I can't see outside. This morning when I woke up, I couldn't see my beautiful view.'

After commiserating with her, I ask where she buys her muesli back home because she'd mentioned how wonderful it is and she seems to know about these things – well, being a lawyer and all.

'From my health food store. There's a really good one on Bondi Road. They make up their own and I add eight almonds. That keeps me going till lunchtime. If I eat rolled oats only, I'm hungry half an hour later.'

To: Kate
From: Mum
Subject: Keeping in touch
Dear Kate:
How are you feeling? Any better? I bought a little something for Spot today.
Your loving mother

To: Mum
From: Kate
Subject: Keeping in touch
dear mum:
i actually feel great today. woke up this morning feeling wonderful. the endorphins must be kicking in. although this afternoon am starting to feel a little tired. bought something already for Spot? if it's clothes, he might outgrow them in six months. how's the holiday going? have you learnt anything new?
love to youuuuuu!!!!!!
Mexxooand spot xxoo

Damian is leading a relaxation class in the gym. The exercise bikes, walkers and weight training equipment are reflected in the full-length mirror at the front of the room. Damian tells us to get a mat from the side of the room and to lie on the floor. There are pillows available too if we want them. Lachlan rushes to get a pillow for my head, although I don't want one, but I use it because he's got it especially and then Ray comes over and lies down beside me. There are about ten people in rows with their feet towards the mirror.

Damian stands over us giving out the instructions. 'Try and keep your awareness on your body, where it is, how it feels. Have an awareness of any thoughts that come into your mind. Be aware of any emotions as you lie here.'

Lying there, I wonder if there's anything that I really like about Lachlan. He did say that it was okay for me to have a second piece of Christmas cake on New Year's Eve. Indulge yourself, he'd said.

A hot still morning. The sun now high in the sky. The leaves on the trees barely moving through the window of the dining room at lunchtime.

'How did you meet your boyfriend?' I ask Felicity.

'He's a cab driver. I met him when he drove me home one night and he turned the meter off and we sat and talked outside my house for ages.'

'What did he think of the retreat?'

'He got a bit of a shock when he first arrived and there was Alexandra blocking the hallway with her walking frame. But I'm trying to talk him into coming with me next time. The only problem was when we were lying on my bed having a cuddle – we had our clothes on – the nurse suddenly came barging in through the door. I'd accidentally knocked the emergency call button and she'd come running down from the clinic and raced straight into my room.'

I laugh.

'This is what it will be like when we're all in an old people's home,' she says.

'You mean we'll all come together at meal times? What else is like being in an old people's home?'

'We don't get bathed in kerosene here.'

'But you can have a paraffin facial.'

We nod in agreement.

In the aerobics class, Damian tells us that if we want to make it harder, we need to wave our arms around more. He turns the music up on the small black tape recorder on the floor. 'But whatever you do, do it with control,' he says.

'Make sure you've got great posture all the way through. Hold in those stomach muscles. Feet wide apart, toes out, abdominal tilt. Exhale down, shoulders down. A soppy number to start with. Lift and reach. Back and over. Reach and over. Other side. And again. Left. One more time. Feet out wide. Side to side. Left left. Keep going. 5,4,3,2. Left. Over. That's it. Back with 4, 3, 2. Arms up and over. Push. Eight more. 8,7,6,5,4,3,2,1.

'Power walking around the room as fast as you can. Have a drink, do up your shoelaces. Now's the time to do it. The slower walkers on the inside, the fast walkers on the outside. That's it. One more lap. Go, team. It will bring your heart rate up, your heart rate down. Time for some abdominal work. Roll yourselves down. Breathing out. Breathing in. Keep your back flat. Your tail on the ground. One more time. One, two, three and four.'

On the way out of the gym, we throw our used towels into a cane basket by the door then line up for a drink at the filtered water cooler.

A woman with very long legs comes up to me. 'You did that class with vigour,' she says.

The lounge room is quite comfortable with its big lounge chairs, ceiling fan, a piano in the corner. The woman who is giving an after-dinner lecture on the uses of aromatherapy oils stands in front of the empty fireplace as we take our places on the lounges.

Ray sits on my right and Lachlan has placed himself on the left so when the oils are passed around for sampling Ray passes on the left saying, and…and then I pass it to Lachlan, who gives me a significant look and touches my hand gently each time. But maybe I'm imagining the significance.

When buying the Goddess Oil in the retreat shop after the lecture, Lachlan stands next to me and I feel self-conscious when I have to say my room number. He says his room number when he purchases some oil for his stuffed-up nose. Ray is standing there too. When Lachlan asks if I'd like to go for a walk, I accept his invitation but wish I was kind and generous enough to include Ray. But still…it's every man for himself around here.

'It would be nice to go for walks at night back home,' says Lachlan as we walk around the block. 'Like in Centennial Park.'

'They close the park at night in Centennial Park. The gates close at five.'

Lachlan dismisses this remark with a wave of his hand.

At breakfast, Felicity and I eat cereal and fruit, drink fresh orange juice and are deciding whether to have seconds of the kiwis and strawberries.

'I'm ready to go back to bed,' says Felicity. 'But I've got a fitness assessment booked for nine.' She wipes the corners of her mouth with the white linen serviette and picks up her cabin key. 'What did you do yesterday?'

'A gym circuit class in the morning, a massage in the afternoon and then a lovely aromatherapy bath.'

'What kind of massage did you have?'

'Chinese. But I think I prefer the feel of skin on skin. Hands on the body.'

'I'd find it really embarrassing to have a young good-looking masseur,' Felicity says.

'Why?'

'I'd be self-conscious about my body.'

'I love having a male masseur. I like a bit of testosterone around the place.'

Felicity smiles but says nothing.

'They can't see your breasts and you can leave your underwear on. They don't even get to see your stomach.'

'But there'd be other bits of fat sticking out that I wouldn't want them to see.'

An overcast day. Streaks of blue sky between flat white clouds. Women in white aprons replenish the containers of hot food in the dining room at lunchtime.

When I join a table, I sense the others inspecting my plate of food. 'I noticed you all looking at my huge plate of food when I sat down,' I say.

'It was so artistically arranged,' says the woman next to me. 'I wondered actually how you managed to fit so much on it. I'd leave a trail of food behind me if I did that.'

'See, I knew you were all staring at my plate of food.'

The woman apologises and insists they weren't making any judgements. Then the whole table compares notes about what treatments they had that morning, which ones they had booked for the afternoon and what they think of the operators.

'My facial with the aromatherapist tomorrow is good timing,' I say. 'I'll ask her to use oils to balance my hormones. The deluxe facial this morning was more irritating than enjoyable. I just wanted the woman to take her hands off me. Her touch was too light and she didn't seem to know what she was doing – especially on the feet. Stupid little feathery strokes – more for a sexual turn-on than a massage. I wanted to say, Get your hands off me, so I could get out of there.'

'I felt the same,' says a woman with a beauty business in Canberra. 'I was thinking how long is this going to go on. I felt like slapping her across the face, those stupid light irritating strokes.'

'Cabin fever,' says another woman.

'You were still running at the end of the class,' says the woman with the long legs in an accusing tone as she nods in my direction. 'I'd flaked out.'

To my relief, the table conversation moves on to the experience of having dental work without anaesthetic.

'What does Sumi look like?' I ask Felicity. 'I've booked in for a special myofacial release with him and I don't know who he is. Even though it costs extra, Lachlan said it's not to be missed.'

'Sumi is a small thin man.'

'He's not that small,' disagrees Ray.

'It's all comparative. Or is the word relative?'

Felicity and I look at each other and smirk.

To: Kate

From: Greatmother

I'm glad you asked if I've learnt anything. The things I've learnt so far are: to keep nuts in the fridge, rice only lasts for a day, don't drink with meals because it dilutes the digestive juices, your digestive system slows down as you get older.

The aquarobics in the pool with Damian are great fun. Damian has the perfect personality for the job. I don't really get a good enough workout here, though, and Damian's classes are very boring and repetitive. And the gym room here is too small and too hot, the equipment not what I'm used to.

Apart from that, all is well, although I'm constantly ravenous. Obviously missing my comfort foods.

Thank God for my tea bags.

What about you? How are you coping with the nausea? Grapes were my saviour when I was pregnant with you. I took them into the office and ate them at my desk with my feet in a basin of cold water to stop the swelling.

Any more spotting?

To: Mum

From: Kate

all's well. no spotting for a week now.

how's the new romance?

After a night-time walk, Lachlan and I sit in the reception area near the air conditioner. The only problem is that now we're back and having a cup of ginger tea, I find it stressful sitting here in silence with him. Fanning myself with a retreat brochure from the display stand, I realise what it is that I dislike the most about him. When I said I suffer from the heat, he acted like I'm having a big whinge when in fact the temperature is forty degrees. He doesn't validate anything I say. Maybe Felicity will join us for a walk tomorrow night.

This time, I don't wait politely till he's drunk his tea. After drinking mine, I excuse myself and leave him in the deserted foyer and walk alone in the dark back to my room.

The sound of the ceiling fan, the bellbirds outside and the scent of lavender from the oil burner as the massage progresses. It's wonderful, this cross between a facial and a full body massage that Jean is giving me. Fabulous. Jean started with firm but relaxing manipulation of the feet, then the chest, neck, face and head.

Jean and I are chatting about this and that during the massage treatment until somehow we get on to the topic of sex.

'Men over fifty aren't interested in sex any more,' says Jean in an authoritative voice. 'They become lazy. It's too much of an effort and men go through a menopause at fifty just like women do. After menopause, women's sexual appetite decreases and so does men's. But you don't hear about it because women aren't going to say they have no sex because they worry that people will think their husbands have lost interest in them – that they don't find them attractive any more.'

Jean talks about her divorce and says she remarried after only eight months on her own. 'I was having a ball,' she says as she tissues the cream off my face. 'I didn't expect that I'd fall in love again, but I did. And you never remarried?'

'No. I never met anyone I was that interested in. There's luck and timing in these things. And I'm fussy and also intolerant. But I do think about it. I miss having an intimate relationship with a man.'

'There's no intimacy if you are with a man.'

'What do you mean?'

'No sex. Once they get to fifty, they lose interest.'

'Really? I didn't know that. Although a married friend said to me recently that sex is a distant memory for men and women our age. I was shocked. I didn't know. No one says that. You don't read about it in articles or in novels.'

'People don't talk about it. I only know because I see so many people in the intimate setting of a treatment room. People talk in this setting and I hear it all the time.'

'So the women still want sex and the men don't?'

'That's right. The men think it's too much trouble. Although it's not always the case. My cousin's husband died at seventy-three while having sex – or just after. He always said it's the way he'd want to go. He still liked to have sex every three days. But it was a mechanical thing with him. He'd just climb on and that was it.'

'Is it because the men can't get erections any more – impotent?'

'No. They're just not interested. You get more sex as a single person.'

'You mean have flings?'

'Yes. Go out and do what feels good. What are you saving it for? Sleep with them on the first date if you want to. If it feels good, do it. That's what I tell my daughters. My husband is shocked. He's very old-fashioned.'

It's still an hour till dinner and it's so hot I've got the fan on maximum, but it doesn't help. This morning, Damian, the gym instructor, led the bushwalk down to the Nepean River and showed us the wombat burrows/holes.

'Why have the wombats left?' I asked him.

'Maybe they found a better burrow elsewhere. Or the wombat children said there wasn't enough room.'

'Or the wombats died.'

'Most likely that.'

Lachlan said that where he stays for a holiday sometimes, the couple who live there take in orphaned wombat babies whose mothers have been killed on the highway and they feed them and give them milk from the bottle. 'They're just like us,' he said.

'I heard that the bellbirds were introduced to this area. That they're not natives. Is that true?'

'I don't know about that,' said Damian. 'I'm a jack of all trades and master of none.'

On the way back from the walk, I stayed at the back with Damian, Lachlan and Ray. The younger women led the way at the front.

The caramel aroma of baked vegetables from the dining room. Around the table we're talking about sex, sex and marriage, sex and single life.

'Marriage is one long monotony,' contributes one woman.

'If they're single, we wonder, how often are they doing it? And with whom? Is he or she good in bed, whatever that means?'

I remember a quote by Auden and decide to make a contribution to the discussion. 'W.H. Auden once described sexual craving as an intolerable neural itch.'

There are nods and sniggers and exclamations of agreement. Then, from across the table, a curvaceous woman in a black plunging shoestring top tells us she believes in the power of witchcraft. 'Witchcraft is one of the few mystical paths where sensuality and sexuality go hand in hand,' she says. 'I have a shower, light some mint incense, stand naked in front of the mirror and say, "You are a goddess, your body is your temple," then do deep breathing exercises.'

No one comments.

'I'm a great tree-hugger,' adds the woman, now enthusiastic about sharing a little more of herself and her ideas. 'Whenever I see a tree, I hug it.'

'Whatever for?'

'I'm saying hello to the spirit who lives inside.'

'Then what?'

'It picks me up. Gives me energy.' She dabs the corners of her mouth. 'Friends nagged me to find a soulmate, so I filled my glass with crushed ice and sliced orange and wrote down the words "I am ready". I bit the orange, focused on the ice and within two hours Gianfranco walked through the door. Six months later, we married.'

The only sound is cutlery scraping against china.

We're listening to a talk by Dana on Understanding Your Natural Shape. The room is full. All the chairs are taken and some people stand against the wall at the back of the room. This small lecture room out the back is air-conditioned so possibly some people have come along to hear the talk because it's one of the few cool places to be in the whole place.

Dana is a small-boned woman, probably in her forties, dressed in loose flowing trousers and top. Afterwards I go up to her to have a chat about the contributing factor of age-related weight gain.

'Midlife is another phase of our lives,' Dana advises, pulling at the sash around her slim waist. 'The whole weight thing, women and body shapes and middle-age spread. It's not only women. Men go through it too. They lose their hair, develop a paunch.' She looks over at Lachlan. 'You're lucky. You've kept your hair.'

He smiles at her.

Later when Lachlan and I are walking around the block on our now regular after-dinner constitutional, I comment on Dana's attractive appearance.

'I think Dana's hands are full of character,' he says.

'What do you mean?'

He doesn't answer. 'Did you see her hands?' he asks after a silence.

'What about them?'

'They're full of character,' he repeats.

How annoying it is that he can't express or articulate any distinguishing features about her hands.

'What was it you liked about her hands? The shape, the colour, the texture?'

'They were full of character.'

It's clear to me I need a man who can express himself.

After a dreadful night of disjointed dreams, I get up and open the curtains. The terror of the last dream is still with me. Suffocating down the bottom of a deep hole in the ground that I'd offered to dig to replant an uprooted tree. I was down the hole trying to get the roots of the large tree into place when I looked up and saw the huge dark shape of the tree looming above me. I realised that there wasn't much air left in the hole and that I'd be dead soon. I called out for help, but in a soft voice because I didn't want to use up too much oxygen. No one heard. I breathed a shallow breath, knowing I wouldn't last very long without air.

It's dusk, the sky turning pink and grey as Lachlan and I sit by the Nepean River getting bitten by sandflies. He asks me why my parents fought. What a dumb question, I think. And then he says something stupid like 'You decided to throw your husband in?' His sniffing and coughing is getting on my nerves. When I said how nice Felicity is, he said some old-fashioned thing like 'A pleasant enough girl.' Last night he told me he lived in England for three years before he got married but he didn't travel or have any love affairs. He went there to study and that was that. He said he got glandular fever three times from overwork, but said it in such a way as if he thought he deserves a medal for hard work.

'You're a slow learner,' I said as a joke and hit him softly on the arm to make my point.

He hit me straight back, but not playfully. I rubbed my arm where it hurt. Arsehole.

'I think masseurs have a perfect life,' he says now. 'They just work when they feel like it,' a note of bitterness in his voice. 'What a life!'

'If massage really appeals to you, you should go and do a course,' I suggest.

'It's no way to earn a living. If you don't work, you don't get paid.'

'No. I meant for you to think about doing it part-time as well as your normal job. One or two nights a week to start with.'

He turns away, his jaw clenched, the muscles on the side of his face working. He doesn't seem interested in my advice.

To: Kate

From: Mum

Hello darling:

I've decided he's really boring. He's a workaholic and has no interests and so I spend my time trying to avoid him now. He used to come and sit at my table, but last night I made an excuse not to go on the walk with him so he didn't come and sit next to me at breakfast time. What a relief!

How are you feeling today?

To: Mum

From: Kate

feel very tired, not much to do at work which doesn't help. almost past the three-month mark.

the thing is with u is that u tend to meet someone and you're interested in them but you don't really know them. that's the problem. good luck with the rest of the holiday. you'll be right mate!

The trolley with vegetable juices for the 'juices only' people squeaks to a halt in the corridor. In the dining room Felicity says it's good to have a whinge and a gossip. I'd been 'whingeing' about one of the beauty practitioners and then apologised for bringing negativity into the room.

'Don't worry,' Felicity says. 'It's bonding when you have a good whinge.'

Other women at the table agree and then they get on to the subject of personal growth courses and begin to exchange stories of their experiences.

Felicity says she's got a horrible story to tell. 'It's about when I did a Forum class and a young man next to me stood up to tell a story about himself. I wished he'd never told us.' She sighs deeply before speaking again.

The other women at the table put their cutlery down and all eyes turn towards Felicity as they wonder what horrible story they're about to hear.

'It's about when he used to babysit for the family next door. He stood up in front of the hundreds of people in the Forum group and shared how when he used to babysit for these people who lived next door he used to suck the baby's penis.'

Every woman at the table gasps in horror except one who says that she'd heard it was not uncommon for Greek grandmothers to do this to their grandsons.

'People were standing up in Forum sessions and saying those sorts of things all the time,' says another woman. 'They had a bank of phones and you were encouraged to ring up people in the breaks – people who you'd had issues with…'

'My daughter rang me to tell me she loved me,' I say. 'She rang me to say that she didn't like me when she was a teenager but she'd got past that stage and that she loved me now and she realised she hadn't told me so.'

'You know the head of the Orange People is in jail now, the one with the ten Cadillacs?' says Felicity..

'And Werner Erhard absconded in the middle of the night with millions of dollars. These people don't want to help other people, they just want to have a big yacht and cruise the Caribbean.'

'That's why this place is so good. It's a not-for-profit organisation.'

To: Kate
    From: Mum

Did you have a quiet day yesterday? We talked about Forum at lunchtime. What do you think about it now?

To: Mum

From: Kate

Subject: Forum

dear mum:

yesterday cleaning, shopping, cooking that sort of stuff. very tired now.

i got heaps out of Forum. every day it impacts on my life. i think about how it's your view of what happens to you or what people say to you. it's the story you put around it. your story.

Through the window the sun burns out of a cloudless blue sky. Time for a meditation session with Sumi in the little room out the back. The seats fill up quickly in the air-conditioned room. We try to keep the door closed but more people keep walking in and leave the door open and the hot air comes in.

Eventually when the room is full and people are even sitting on the floor with their backs against the wall, Sumi explains how it's important to be able to be the watch tower on the hill and to watch ourselves meditate. Ten minutes of silent meditation. Then it's all very embarrassing when we have to do some gibberish with our eyes closed and then pretend to drop down dead.

'The feeling in the pit of my stomach was laughter,' I say to Felicity when we had to drop down dead. 'Laughter welling up. It all seemed so serious I just wanted to laugh.'

'It was the same for me.'

'The oming didn't go so well. Ar, or, mm.'

'We were all too self-conscious.'

'You can make a noise,' Sumi had said when I'd started to cry in the myofacial release session. 'You don't have to be silent. Do you know what the sadness is about?'

'It was the way you said, "Let go of your arm. I'll look after it for you. Don't feel you have to move it for me. I'll take care of it."'

'It's okay to laugh,' he'd said earlier when he was flapping my arm around and I was trying hard to suppress the laughter.

At the end of the session, he opens his arms to me. Asks if I'd like a hug. Stepping right up to him, I remind myself not to cling when I hug him. I wait for him to be the one who releases the hug first. Before I leave the room, he suggests I have a conversation with my arm to find out what the pain in the arm is all about.

Walking back to my room, I inhale the fragrant basil and rosemary of the herb garden. Lachlan is lying on a banana chair under a palm tree reading a book near the swimming pool. He's wearing long trousers and a shirt. Obviously his going-home clothes. I stop and thank him for recommending a treatment with Sumi. He does not respond to my gratitude. Cold and uncommunicative would be a good description of his attitude towards me. We never did get to tell each other what we do for a living.

Back in my room, I turn the radio on. Real estate specialist John McGrath is advising listeners to buy the best-quality house and the best position they can.

That same day my friend Simon arrives at the retreat to give two lectures: 'Weight Release' and 'Happiness – It's Your Heritage'. By coincidence he is given the room that Lachlan has just vacated.

Afterwards, Simon suggests we drive to the café down the road for a coffee. Simon pulls up on the gravel outside the Federation-style cottage. We sit outside on the wooden balcony rather than inside but the flies around our faces are persistent and relentless. A waitress in jeans and T-shirt comes out of the front door carrying a plate of pastries for the table of women beside us.

Simon uses both his hands to wave the flies away. 'Did you come here often during the week?' he asks.

'No, I never got in my car for the whole week. I didn't feel the need to leave the retreat. Apart from going for walks at night time. It was too hot to be outside.'

'Maybe we should have sat inside,' he says with irritation. 'These flies are driving me mad.'

'It's nice to be outside.'

'Did you go cycling? There are great places to cycle round here.'

'No. It was too hot to go anywhere. I stayed close to the air conditioner in Reception most of the time.'

'So do you think you'd come here again?'

'Maybe for a weekend, but not for a week.'

'You really did come here at the wrong time of the year. You could have stayed at home enjoying the sea breezes.'

The flies are trying to crawl into the orifices of my nose, my ears, my eyes. I wave them away. 'Flies. Flies. Flies. Bloody flies.'

Acknowledgements

First published in *Quadrant*:
'Art and the Mermaid', 'After the Rain', 'Around Midnight', 'JM',
'The Backpack', 'Undulations', 'On Valentine's Day', 'Alfresco',
'Jean-Pierre', 'At the Festival', 'Aunt Helen', 'Towards the End', 'The
New Baby', 'Tell Me About What Happened On New Year's Eve'.

First published in *Overland*:
'After the Games', 'Around the World in Fifty Steps'.

'It's Pot Luck When You Move Into a Unit',
winning entry UTS Alumni Short Story Competition 2014,
first published in *UTS Writers Connect*